EMOTIONALLY CHARGED

Second Edition
Published by Fairies and Fantasy Pty Ltd 2011
Paperback ISBN: 978-0-6485427-6-6
Hardcover ISBN: 978-1-922390-12-7

www.selinafenech.com

EMOTIONALLY CHARGED

THE EMPATH 1 CHRONICLES

SELINA A. FENECH

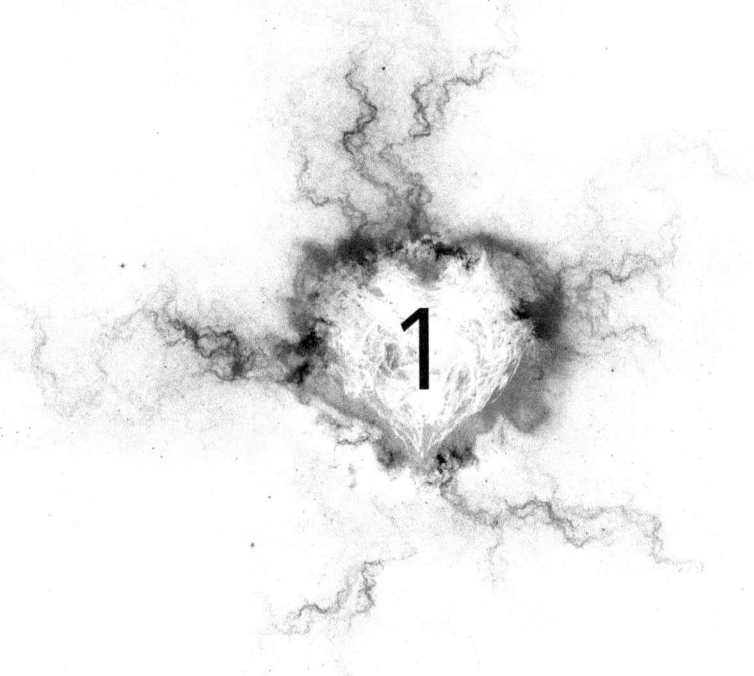

1

stared at the crack that ran up our living room wall. The ground had stopped shaking, but tremors still zinged through my body. *Did that really just happen?*

I couldn't drag my eyes away from that lightning-shaped fracture scarring the wall. Apart from the contents of our shelves that were now on the floor — books, ornaments, a plaster "Olivia" I'd painted when I was five, now smashed to bits — it seemed to be the only visible damage. I should probably have been upset by it, but instead I felt... *excited.* The crack gave me shivers like it was carved up my spine. *That really just happened.*

The floor rumbled under my feet and I shared a look with Mom and Dad, all three of us ready to bolt out of the home we'd just re-entered after fleeing for the first time.

The aftershock passed before we could move. Just the last little ripple after the wave.

We'd always known our town was near a major fault, but it was one of those sleepy fault lines that didn't do anything for decades, centuries even. Then just when everyone in our middle-class paradise had achieved a false sense of security, here it was, throwing a great big earthquake at us.

Dad talked on the phone to his cop buddy to get all the details and updates. He repeated the news out loud for Mom and me to hear.

"Power's out everywhere, and Terry doesn't think they'll get it back on any time soon."

Mom had already gathered up her collection of scented candles, those that hadn't broken in a fall, and lit them. Her first course of action in any blackout. The whole room smelled of struck matches and ylang ylang.

"Mom, it's not even dark yet."

"They make me feel better," she said, shrugging and lighting the last one.

Dad put his hand over the phone and looked at Mom

seriously. "Terry says there have been reports of people looting."

Mom paused a moment, then stomped into the kitchen and picked up a brush and dustpan. "The kind of person who would take advantage of a situation like this deserves their own personal karmic earthquake."

My imagination teased me with scenes of what could be happening out on the streets. Broken buildings where looters, police officers, and emergency response crews played their roles. I imagined a world of adventure outside. Bad guys and heroes. *Handsome* heroes.

Mom was always pushing me to follow my dreams, but truthfully, the only things I wanted were fantasies. Damseling for a gorgeous superhero, escaping to a magical world with a fairy prince, being adored by a morally vague vampire: I'd take any of the above. In real-life terms, I didn't know what I wanted. I just knew if I ever got a chance to follow my fantasy dreams I'd be there with bells on. Real life was kind of dull, and maybe an earthquake wasn't the romantic escapism I normally went for, but I could work with it. Even a sexy fireman would suffice.

I daydreamed as I kneeled down next to Mom where she worked at brushing up shattered ornaments that had fallen from our shelves. Her collection of ceramic owls would never be the same. I helped pick up the few which had broken into larger pieces and put them aside. Mom loved her owls. Maybe some could be glued back together.

Dad's news report continued. "We were lucky. A lot of people have lost homes. And the old post office is flattened, but we've been expecting it to fall down for years. How many times did I try to tell the council to get it renovated?"

Mom counted on her fingers and Dad added his own fingers into the count too while he listened to the phone again. "There's a shelter being set up in Livvy's high school for anyone whose house is unsafe."

I bet they needed volunteers. The shaken world felt full of possibility and I wanted to be part of it. Even handing out blankets had my mind brewing up dreams of romance. Mopping at the brow of a dust covered EMT who'd just saved a puppy from a crumbled home...

I have to get out there. "Mom, can I go and help at the school?"

Mom looked up at me. A glow of pride and the darkness of worry showed all over her face.

I could read the emotions clear as subtitles. For as long as I could remember, I'd been able to see energy shining from a person with their emotions. Not like an aura or anything; that sounded so New Age woo-woo. I was just good at knowing how people felt. Always had been. It was my one and only superpower. When I was a kid, I used to dress up and play at being a caped crime fighter, Awesome Olivia. Then I'd realized reading someone's feelings wasn't the kind of power that was useful in a fist fight. But it did come in handy sometimes.

I pre-empted the inevitable worried mom speech with soothing words. "I'll just be helping out in a shelter, under the watchful eye of aid workers, responsible adults and doctors. Probably the safest place at the moment, right?"

"You know I like to let you make your own choices but things sound pretty rough out there. I don't want you to get hurt." She looked at the dustpan and brush in her hands as though making a point about the damage the earthquake had done. Her startling blue eyes turned back toward me. Why couldn't I have inherited those? My eyes were brown instead, to match my hair which she guilted me out of dyeing. Harsh chemicals didn't fit her idea of green living.

I could win *this* debate though. "Just think how appealing some volunteer work will look on my college application as an extracurricular activity. And I can swing past your shop and make sure it's okay."

"I hope there's not too much damage. I just had a porcelain shipment come in. Great timing, right? I'd go check myself but there's so much to do here." She paused, chewed at her bottom lip. "All right, off you go then, but be careful."

Dad finished his phone call and kissed the top of my head when I stood up, his moustache tickling my forehead. "I think it's a beautiful idea, Lollipop. Good on you for wanting to help out."

Mom walked over to empty her dustpan, sighing as shattered owls tumbled into the trash. Shards of pink rolled in and I knew it was the remains of her favorite one. Dad gave her a hug as though they were standing by the grave of a beloved relative.

I saw how sad Mom was and gave her a peck on the cheek. "Thanks, Mom. I'll be careful. And I'll keep an eye out for any owls needing adoption on my way." I threw on my red trench coat, chucked my phone, keys and wallet in the pockets, and headed for the door.

"Buses are still running, Livvy," Dad called out. "There's a clear route to your high school. Just a couple of hours, okay? Be safe."

"Of course," I replied. "See you soon."

The air outside had a hint of dust and sense of silent awe. People filled the street, gossiping in relieved whispers. A hairline crack across a nearby pavement had drawn the attention five or so local kids, who stared at it the way I had stared at the one in my home—as though it could snap open like a monster's maw at any second and engulf me.

Sirens sounded in the distance.

The possibilities of what could happen tonight, and an intense desire for adventure ... or *something* ... made my body hum. I pulled my trench coat tight around me and set off.

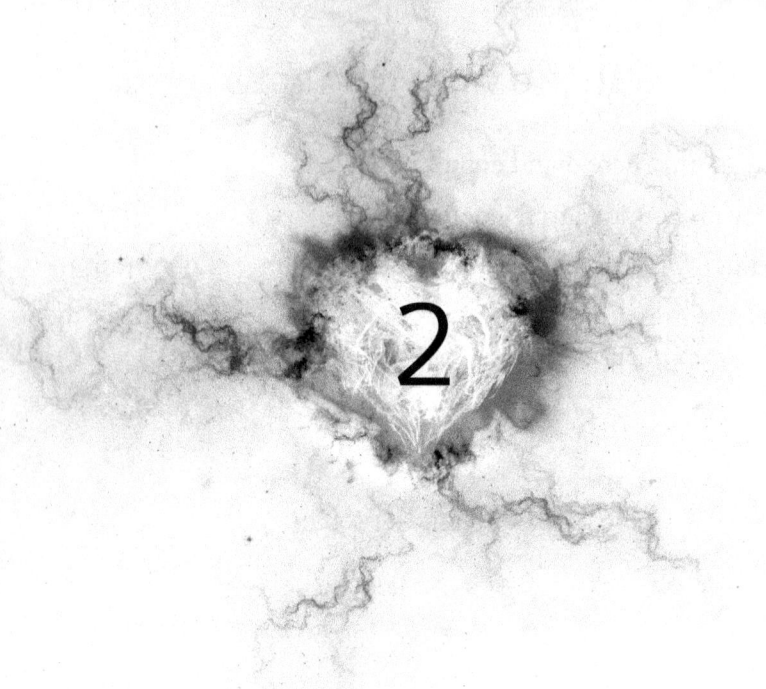

2

his. This was what I was made for. I felt like I was actually glowing or vibrating, or something.

"Bless. You're just an angel." A woman with a cloud of white hair patted my hand as she took a blanket from me. She smiled, but I felt the tremble in her palm and sensed her fear.

It made me tingle.

I felt like some kind of weirdo. These people were here because their homes were too unsafe to stay in, or gone entirely. I saw fear and sadness on every face, *felt it* in my bones, and there I was, bubbling over on some kind of weird high.

What is wrong with me?

EMOTIONALLY CHARGED

I'd felt it before I'd even reached the shelter. On the bus ride, a buzz had built in me the closer I'd got to the school and it'd been non-stop since. I wasn't sure how many blankets I'd handed out or how many people I'd escorted into the gym, finding them a patch of ground to rest on. Any injured went straight to the hospital, but I still felt like a warrior helping out in the aftermath of a battle. Handsome heroes so far had been non-existent, sadly. I remained hopeful and kept busy. I'd listened to people's stories of the earthquake, dragged restless children back to their parents, and helped unload the cartons of bottled water the local U-Mart trucked in. The cartons felt feather-light—I was on such a high. *I'll probably be aching tomorrow.* I'd tripped over twice, my feet wanting to move faster than I could keep up with, and my hands twitched and jittered. It was probably adrenaline. Maybe I needed to take a break.

I found my way to the volunteer's area and cracked open a bottle of water. I squeezed it too hard as I was drinking and splashed water all over my chest. *Well at least it's a perfect set up for a meet-cute.* I held my breath, wishing this was the moment my hero would appear and be enamored by my clumsiness. But the only man approaching was my history teacher. I sighed and patted myself dry with paper towels.

Trevor was also the coordinator for the shelter. Any other

day he was Mr. Jones, but today he insisted on being Trevor. He leaned on a bench next to me and pushed the sweat up off his forehead and back over his head, slicking graying hair away from his face.

"Thanks for all your help tonight, Olivia." His voice came out as a long sigh. "I wish I still had a teenager's stamina. Is this your first break? You've been at it for hours."

Hours? It felt like twenty minutes, tops. My eyes popped wide. "What's the time?"

I pulled my phone from my pocket for the first time and saw it was half past eleven. I also saw three missed calls and two texts from my mom, and a couple from my BFF Nati. *I should have checked in with her. Where is my head tonight?* Maybe it wasn't me buzzing, just my phone doing its vibro-dance in my pocket.

Trevor watched me with concern as I grimaced. "Sure you're okay?"

"I'll be fine, as long as my parents don't kill me." I tapped the screen to call them back and got nothing but failed calls. No bars meant no signal. The messages left by my parents were all from back before seven o'clock. The last bus ran at ten-thirty, and thanks to my parents' hippy car-free household policy, last bus translated to curfew and I knew it. *Especially* on the evening of a mid-level natural disaster. I was going to find myself on the wrong end of a serious lecture, assuming I could find a way home.

Trevor watched my hopeless phone poking. "Phone towers have battery backups which work for a couple of hours, but in a long blackout like this they will have cut out by now."

Even if I could get through, I had no way to get home that wasn't going to put out the neighbors, or worse, Terry. I cringed. A ride with him in his cop car was not the way I wanted to arrive home.

Maybe I could stay in the shelter for the night. I just had to let my parents know I was here and safe.

"Sorry Mr. um... Trevor. I sort of maybe kind of missed my ride home."

Trevor looked around the gym. Everyone was settled in, many asleep already. Even half the volunteers had curled up in a corner somewhere as the influx of new people had slowed down. "I could ask around for a lift for you, or—"

"I'm happy to stay."

He sighed. "Yes, fine, you can stay, if you can find a spare blanket and bit of floor. Landlines are still working if you want to use the phone in the office to let your parents know. Briefly. Have to keep the line clear for official calls."

"Do you think you could call them for me?" I hated talking

on the phone. I couldn't see people's reactions, couldn't tell how they were feeling and always ended up saying the wrong thing, even at the best of times. And now was far from the best of times. "It would just be better if a teacher told them, instead of me. You know, someone of authority."

And yes, I was also dodging the lecture.

Trevor rubbed his forehead, the pen still in his hand marking it blue. He added my name to his clipboard. "Go on. I'll call them. School's off for the week and people are going to be here a while, so if you want to help out again tomorrow everyone would appreciate it."

Sounded like an offer I couldn't refuse. I nodded gratefully and he took down my number and left for the office to make the call.

I still had my phone in my hand, and voice mail was down so I checked the texts my mom had sent. The earliest must have been while I was still on the way in—Mom reminding me of the bus schedule. The next, five minutes after the first, asked me to check the boxes of new stock that had just arrived at her shop.

I'd missed the bus home *and* I had completely forgotten to go past her shop on the way in like I'd told her I would. *I can't believe I spaced so bad. The winner of daughter of the year? Not me.*

I *could* still go now. Real quick, just zip out and back before anyone noticed I was gone.

Heading out onto the streets seemed a bit crazy but I really wanted to do this for Mom. Knowing her "Duck Egg Blue" home-wares boutique was okay would mean a lot to her, especially after she'd lost her owls. Her little shop wasn't far from school. Normally a ten-minute walk, but tonight I felt like I could fly.

Another family trudged into the hall armed with pillows and suitcases, prepared to camp out with everyone else, looking sad and lost. I felt bad for them, but there were other volunteers who would help them out. I needed to check on the shop before it got any later and this adrenaline kick I was on ended and I crashed.

I waited until no-one seemed to be watching me and slipped out the gym entrance and through the school gates, and jogged down the street. The chunky heart pendant I wore thudded on my chest like a second heartbeat.

Just checking on Mom's shop, I repeated to myself, while a deeper, quieter voice whispered of heroes and adventure and what-if.

If only I'd remembered that with adventure, comes danger.

3

Once away from the school, where generators were running and floodlights lit up every corner of the grounds, it was quiet.

I hadn't ever seen the town so deserted. The police weren't even out driving around. They must have had a lot more on their plate than patrol. It was quieter than any other time I could remember.

Mom always called the town 'sleepy'. On this night, though, I would call it beyond sleepy. It had an almost post-apocalyptic feel.

In reality, there were still plenty of buildings standing and no enormous cavern in the middle of the street like there might have been in some end-of-the-world movie. Which probably also meant no grisly-but-good-hearted savior riding in on his motorbike to sweep me to safety. It would have been a lot more interesting if there had been, but for now, I needed to get to Mom's shop and back to school before they noticed I was gone.

For some reason, the details of the older terrace housing which backed the main street appeared clearer than I'd ever seen before, even in the dark. It was like I could see better than normal. I looked around for a full moon or some other light source to explain it, but found nothing. Shame. I felt like I wanted to howl at the moon. I almost giggled at how good I felt and then thought again how strange it was, that I could feel *good* in the midst of such chaos.

No matter how many times Dad had said the post office was going to come crashing down someday, the sight of it as I passed by was eerie. Water flowed from a burst pipe and piles of mail were strewn throughout the wreckage, snow drifts of letters white on the ground.

Slowing my pace, I enjoyed the excitement of the solitary darkness. So I got a bit over-excited tonight and missed my bus, but I helped people tonight and it had felt *amazing*. Mom would understand. She was always understanding and encouraging.

Checking her shop out was the least I could do.

She loved her shop like she loved her owl collection. When I was younger, she'd talked about getting a real owl. I'd looked at her like she was crazy. "Ew no, so messy! You have to feed them real meat. So difficult."

"Life should be like that. Difficult, messy, and real," she'd replied. "You have to do what you have to do to make your dreams come true."

Now, I understood what she meant. So maybe it was crazy I wanted a rich, handsome prince to sweep me away to far-off lands of adventure, intrigue and decadence. But I didn't want my life in half measures. I wanted real affluence, real excitement, real romance. Mom's dreams had come true, and I wanted to be as happy and in love as her and Dad one day.

On the main street the shops were all still standing. Some had cracks running up pastel-painted fronts, splitting quirky logos with jagged smiles. The arty mosaic archway leading into the boutique district had crumbled, blocking the road so cars were unable to pass. I felt a pang of grief for it, knowing it was a humpty that couldn't be put back together.

A lot of windows were broken, spilling glass onto the street and making the shop displays sparkle as though the shabby chic furniture or gourmet cupcakes had been sprinkled with diamonds.

Then I noticed it wasn't just a lot of windows. It was every window. It made sense the earthquake had broken glass, but just around the corner I hadn't noticed any windows broken on the rows of townhouses.

A beam of light shone out of a building up ahead. I froze. *Someone's in there, but someone good or bad?* I didn't need to see the exact pastel shade of the shop to know it was Duck Egg Blue. The light jiggled, then vanished. The sound of shattering porcelain echoed in the street followed by a boy-like chuckle.

I'm guessing not good.

"Hey!" The word came out before I stopped to think. "Hey, get out of there!"

The humming inside me had grown louder, anger pulsing through my veins. *That's my mom's shop.* The hell I was going to let someone trash or loot it. Getting called out should make them run away.

The possibility it wouldn't only struck me when four figures in hoodies jumped out through the cleared window, bringing with them an avalanche of retro dinner sets from the display. I cringed as plates smashed on the pavement.

The gang turned my way and I saw they were just boys, younger than me. I didn't recognize them from school, and they didn't dress like teens from this area either. More like kids from the housing estate a couple of 'burbs over who sometimes crashed parties around here. The kind of kid Mom always told me to be understanding of. They had tougher situations than we did, but it was hard to be understanding when they were smashing up my mom's livelihood.

Two shone flashlights my way. I squinted into the harsh glare.

I stood taller than a couple of the thugs, but it was still four against one. Why did I feel like I could deal with this? The fizzy high I was on had my confidence up and blocking the part of my mind that knew this could be dangerous, and that feeling of invincibility could just make it worse. A point proved when the boys headed for me instead of making a guilty dash.

"Stay back. I have pepper spray." I bluffed, reaching my hand into a pocket of my trench coat. I grabbed for my phone instead, swiped it on, but couldn't dial on the touch screen without looking, and I wasn't sure the emergency number would even redirect and work with most of the network down. What would they do if they saw me dialing? Back off, or advance faster? It didn't seem worth the risk when it could take ages for the cops to arrive.

"Pepper spray? I eat that stuff on my breakfast," one of them joked.

I took steady steps away as the boys came closer. Every

one was dressed in black, like they were in uniform. They had no distinguishing features visible apart from slightly varying heights. I started imagining being a victim who couldn't identify her attackers and I didn't like it.

I tried to warn them off again. "I'll call the police."

"Relax, we're just out for some fun." He chuckled, the same chuckle I'd heard when he was smashing things in Mom's shop. His idea of fun worried me.

Glass crunched on the concrete footpath behind me. I spun around. Another boy, all in black loomed over me.

He grabbed for my arm. I gasped, stepping quickly out of his reach.

Anger shone from him and my body flared with adrenaline. The five thugs penned me in and took turns pushing at me or grasping for me. I reacted on instinct, my body taking control. I dodged, avoiding a lunge from one side then a snatch from the other. They jeered and taunted, trying to get their hands on me. Fingers wrapped around my arm, but I easily twisted out of them.

But the more I avoided them, the more I saw the anger in them build.

No one had ever been this mad at me before. It scared me. It set my whole body on fire.

"Someone help!" I cried out, but my voice was lost in the wide street. I doubted anyone would hear. No hero would come and save me. This wasn't one of my daydreams. This was a nightmare.

I ducked under a wide swing from the closest guy. He snarled violently. They weren't playing anymore. Remembering my self-defense class, I pulled my keys out of my pocket. I grabbed my phone with the other hand. I made a wild jab at the thug's chest with my longest key while I looked at my phone screen, thumbing in an emergency call.

The key sank into flesh, startling me. I didn't expect it to break skin at all, let alone slide right into him like a dagger. My hand warmed with the guy's blood. *What the heck?*

I paused too long and was shoved in the back.

I fell flat on my face. My phone dropped from my hand and skittered out of reach. On the ground, my mind helpfully recalled the second part of the self-defense lesson emphasizing the importance of disabling your attackers, not just pissing them off even more.

I barely felt the fall, but when I tried to call for help again there was no air in my lungs. Numbly, I registered broken glass jutting out of my palms.

One of the guys grabbed my shoulder and rolled me over.

I snatched his hand in both of mine and twisted. I swear I heard bones break. He screamed.

I also thought I heard footsteps approaching, fast. I might have just been hearing things. Just wishful thinking as the guy cradled his wrist, called me something I wouldn't repeat and kicked me in the side of the head.

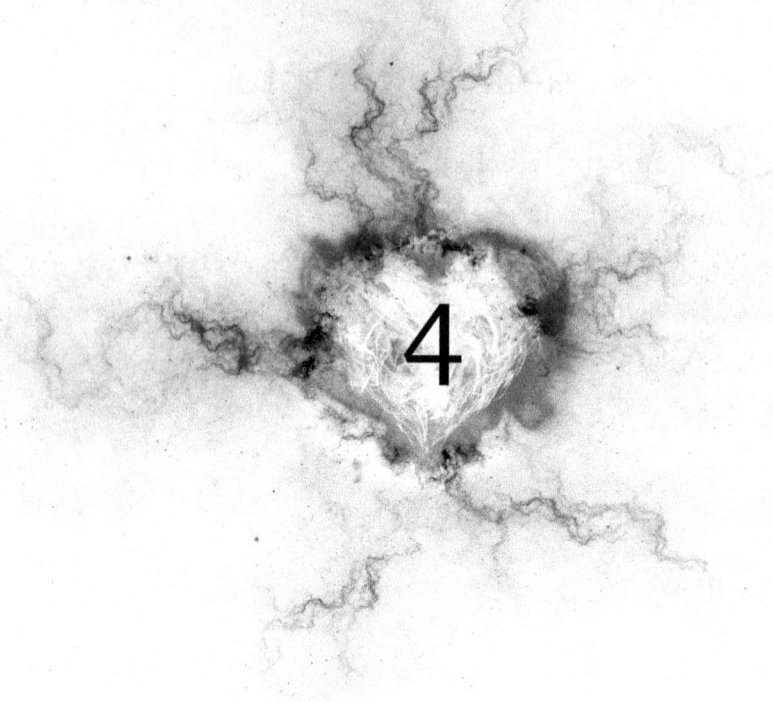

4

My world swam in darkness. Sounds of scuffling faded in and out, and energy surged through my body.

Snapping my eyes open, I watched a man in a white button-down shirt throw one of the hoodies against a power pole. Actually picked him up and *threw* him. The others were already running, or stumbling, away.

Someone had come to save me. It was a miracle.

The kid thrown against the pole slumped there, unmoving. My eyes widened, hoping he was just unconscious.

Dusting his hands, my savior turned around to reveal the face of a male model. I blinked, and in that instant he went from all the way over there to over beside me. I blinked again, confused and unsure of reality. Because now I really had gone into daydream world.

The new guy's shirt accentuated his V-shaped chest like it had been tailored for a perfect fit and his blond hair sat flawlessly as though he hadn't just dealt with a bunch of looting delinquents. His sleeves were rolled neatly below his elbows, and although he only looked about twenty, the watch on his wrist was expensive. I'd seen it in classy magazine ads.

"Are you all right?"

Even his voice was dreamy.

I tried to sit up so I wasn't so awkward and prone, wanting to be more presentable for this god-like figure. "Hngh. Ow. Crap."

Damn it.

The guy chuckled, and his smile made my heart shiver like a nervous bunny. When he grabbed my hands and helped me up with perfect care, I thought I would lose it entirely.

"You were amazing," he said, bending to collect my phone and keys from nearby. "When I heard someone calling for help, I came as quick as I could. Saw most of the fight while I ran down the street. I thought you had them dealt with on your own for a minute. Very impressive."

I groaned, reliving my misguided foray into heroism.

"Impressive like a high-jumping lemming."

He half-smiled. "Cutest lemming I've seen in a while."

Gulp.

He handed my phone and keys back to me, giving me a scrutinizing look. "But really, how do you feel?"

How did I feel? I'd just been thrown on the ground and kicked in the head, but actually I felt... "Good? Does that mean I'm in shock?"

"Maybe. Maybe something better. My name is Jake." He took my hand, gently cleaning blood off it with a tissue, and I forgot to ask what was better or whether I needed a blanket and hot chocolate in case it was shock after all.

"I'm Livvy," I replied, without stuttering, which was the second miracle of the night.

"Let's find you somewhere to recover then, my lovely Livvy."

Guys had tried calling me that before and it had always sounded corny until now. This guy's voice was so tasty I could lick it.

He looped my arm in one of his like a Victorian gentleman and I trotted obediently alongside him. I pretended to need the support more than I did, just to squeeze a little closer. I was going to make the most of this, in case I woke up and discovered it was a concussion-induced dream.

EMOTIONALLY CHARGED

We walked to the end of the street and sat at a bus stop on the corner. It was beautiful, a real work of art. Designed to bookend the archway that used to stand at the other end of the strip, the heavy concrete bench was covered in colorful mosaic tiles.

My mind refused to help me out with anything to say. *Thank you for saving me* was the obvious thing, but it seemed so inadequately lame I couldn't make it come out my mouth. Jake kept looking at me, and I read amusement and satisfaction all over him. *Oh God, he smells so good.* I couldn't say that out loud either.

He broke the silence after what felt like forever, but was more likely only seconds long. "I bet you feel better than good, don't you?"

I shrugged. I did still feel pretty tingly. I looked at my palms, where glass had poked from my skin, and found them clear and clean. What?

Maybe I'd imagined it. My brain had been MIA. "I think I've been on an adrenaline kick most of the night."

He chuckled. "Getting kicked like you did, aren't you surprised you're already feeling okay? You don't realize how fast you were moving back then, do you? And did you know you almost ripped that guy's hand off?"

"I did *what?*"

"It's fine. It was self-defense." Jake paused for a moment. He assessed me with piercing eyes. "What if I said you were more than normal? Something different, better, possibly even supernatural? Would you freak on me or—"

"Would I think it was a dream come true? The latter." I nodded with wide eyes, waiting to see what he'd reveal. I half-expected he was setting me up for some epic punch line, but there was an energy in the air I couldn't deny. A magic I wanted to embrace. And if this guy had the key to that? Dream. Come. True.

Jake pointed his finger at my chest and then his. "You, me—we have superpowers."

Tingles. I eyed him up and down, looking for outward signs of mental illness. But I felt his sincerity and wondered if this was what I'd been waiting for my whole life. If by some miracle my dreams were about to become true. *Things come in threes, right?*

And the things I'd seen him do, the things I had done tonight, were they more than normal? I wasn't one hundred percent sure. It had all been such a blur. "Okay. That sounds great and all, but this is a bit outside the realm of real life. I'm going to need some kind of proof to be onboard here." *Please have proof. Please have proof. Please have proof.*

He raised a perfect eyebrow. "How about a visual demo?"

Jake took my hand and pulled me off the bench. Turning back to it, he gave it a swift kick in the center. The bench cracked down the middle and fell inward in a kaleidoscope of tiles and crumbled concrete. It was as completely destroyed as the archway down the road. The bookends matched even more now.

I stared, mouth open, and he waited for my response with a smile.

"Where are we supposed to sit now?" I giggled, edging on hysteria at the scope of what was happening. "And also, what the how?"

Down the road, headlights broke through the darkness and a car swung around the corner, heading down the street. Jake waved at it and turned back to me.

"You're like me, like us." He gestured to the car, speaking fast as it approached. "You've always been able to read people's feelings, right? You feel stronger when people are angry, or full of energy when others are scared. When emotions surround you, you think faster, move faster, heal faster."

I found myself nodding to his words, realizing what he said was the truth. This wasn't just a dream. I'd always been like that. My one unique feature, hidden on the inside, was more special than I had ever realized. His words repeated in me. *You're like me, like us.*

"It's real. I can tell you feel it. We're empaths. That's why I'm here. We're always on the look-out for other people like us, and the easiest time to find them is during a natural disaster when emotions are heightened across the whole population. It's often the first time empaths really experience their power, like you have tonight."

The black SUV skidded to a stop beside us and the front-side window opened. I couldn't quite see inside but I heard a man talk. "We've been driving 'round looking for you for ages. What's the deal, Jake?"

Jake tilted his head to me and simply said, "Got one."

A girl not much older than me burst out the back door. "You really found one? Zomigosh, it's a girl!" She squealed and came toward me, her shimmering red hair flying around her from her leap out of the vehicle. The front doors opened and two guys stepped out. They were stunning, every one of them. I made an effort to keep my mouth from hanging open.

Everything was happening so fast. I had superpowers. Jake had superpowers. Now I was meeting so many hot people with superpowers.

I reached out a hand to the girl to introduce myself and she wrapped her arms 'round my shoulders, hugging me as she jiggled a little dance. "I thought I might have been the only one. Don't get me wrong, I love my boys, but I've been dying to find another girl 'path."

Jake cleared his throat. "Everyone, this is Livvy. Livvy, that's Emma, over there's Donny." He nodded to the tallest guy, whose velvety black skin rippled with muscles which barely seemed to fit under his clothes. "And this jerk is Jamie." Jake grinned at the last guy, a few years younger than all of them. He and Jake looked like they could be brothers. Jamie gave Jake the finger, smirking all the while, then shook my hand. Donny just nodded silently.

"So, you guys come to natural disaster areas to help out, and hope you find more people like you—like us?" I couldn't believe I was talking to a team of real-life superheroes. I needed to sit down but the bench option had been removed.

"That's pretty much what we do," Jamie said.

"How did Jake find you? How long have you known what you are? Did you already know? Are you from around here?" Emma overflowed with questions and I couldn't find a gap to answer any.

Jake cleared his throat. He leant on Jamie's shoulder and

gave me a bashful smile, threatening to liquidize my legs. "I know you just met us all, and I know it's late, but we'd really like for you to come with us."

I exhaled a little too loudly. "With you? With you where?"

"Just to hang out for a bit, chat some more. I know I unloaded a lot on you all at once. I'd love to talk it over more and explain things properly because there aren't many of us. Empaths need to stick with our kind. We're stronger together. That's why we have our team."

Hang out and chat. I could do that. I had to.

This was really happening. My impossible dreams were coming true, and I had to find out more. I couldn't let these empaths just leave me in my normal life again. My parents weren't expecting me home now and with so much going on at the shelter, I doubted my absence would be noted. I could spend all night with Jake and his team if I wanted. And I *wanted*.

I knew I should be thinking about this more seriously, but I had trouble focusing on anything other than Jake's smile, and the warm feeling it gave me inside. I couldn't sense any dangerous emotions coming from any of the empaths, just warm, happy fuzziness. The desire to jump in the car with them proved overwhelming. "Sure. Let's go."

Jake and Emma beamed. Jamie's smirk remained in place.

Donny didn't show much expression. His face remained still, like the carving of a god. He checked his watch, also expensive. "We're meant to be flying back tonight."

"Oh. In that case..." I hesitated.

"We can chat in a café at the airport until we fly out." Jake looked down at me, his eyelids half closed and a small, pouting smile on his lips. "Come with us."

A rush of warmth flooded me. I felt so secure, so sure. I nodded.

Looking past their attractive forms was difficult, but in their emotions all I read was excitement and pleasure at finding me. They wanted me. I was special. Like them? Maybe not quite, but they wanted me anyway. Jake and his friends didn't feel like strangers at all. They already felt like family, as if I knew them. I trusted them and going with this group, this team, was the only thing in the world I knew I wanted. It could be my only chance to live my dreams. Mom would tell me to go for it.

Somehow we went from chatting in the rental car, to chatting in the airport, to chatting on the plane.

It wasn't the first time I told my parents I'd be in one place but went somewhere else.

But it was the first time that going somewhere else involved a first-class flight.

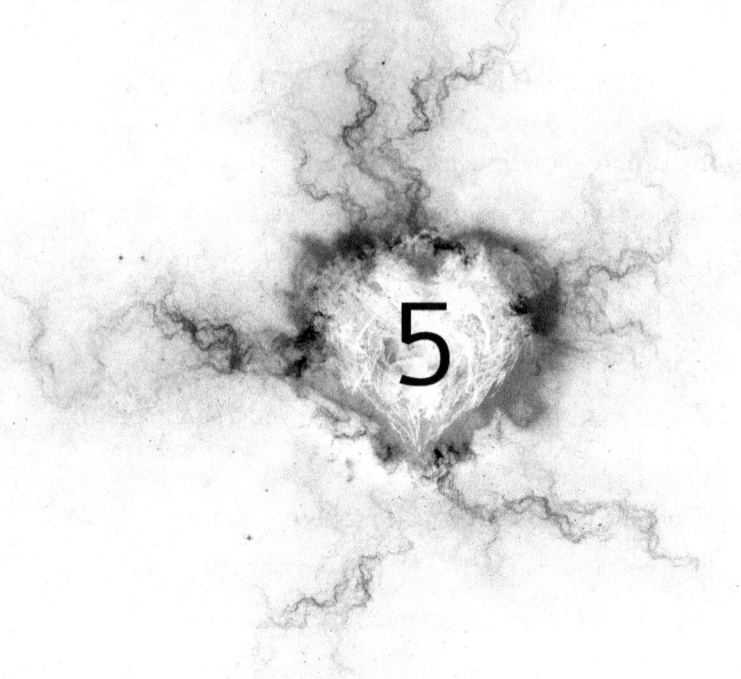

5

First class was *wow*. Everyone treated our group like royalty. Jake sorted out everything and the airline squeezed me onto the flight at late notice. Even with strict airport security we breezed through with the team's excess baggage, no questions asked. Jake reassured me we weren't going far, and they would fly or drive me back home any time I wanted. They only flew up to get to the quake site fast, and were only a few hours' drive away from my Bellscroft.

Why were they leaving my home town so soon? Wasn't there any more they could do for people after the earthquake? Maybe they'd done their sweep and were happy no one was trapped under rubble somewhere. We didn't talk about that at all. Mostly they had questions for me about who I was, and what I knew so far about my abilities. Which I had to admit wasn't much, with that night being my first experience. But I explained how it seemed like I was moving crazy fast and the firey strength I felt, and they all nodded like they knew exactly what I meant. Because they have felt it too. Then they relaxed into the flight as though they had been working hard, and I relaxed alongside them, basking vicariously in their post-heroism glow.

Once off the plane at the airport, I spotted a payphone while Emma was spending fifteen minutes freshening up in the ladies room and Jake was arranging the valet for his car. *I really should call my parents.* My phone battery was way too low, but I had some change in my wallet and had one of my parent's numbers memorized. My mom's cell. When I rang, it went straight to voicemail. Network mustn't be back up at home yet. After the beep, I had no idea what to say either. How could I sum up the events that brought me there?

"Umm, hey, it's me, I'm fine. Don't worry, everything is fine and I'll call you again soon to explain." I hung up, hoping they'd get the message soon. I worried about them being worried, but then Emma was back and Jake was there again too and my whole world turned sunny again.

If the flight was decadent, their house was something from a fairy tale. Not a house. An abso-frikkin'-amaze-balls mansion. Not too old-fashioned, not too modern. Perfectly classy. It was mid-morning by the time we got there and the sun sparkled off the building like a dream. *I wonder which one of them has the trust fund. Probably all of them.*

At first sight of the mansion, all I could do was splutter like I'd spontaneously learned another language. "Ung, thas, wha?"

This was luxury on a level I'd never imagined. No, that wasn't true. It was luxury on the level I daydreamed about every day but never dared think I'd experience. I'd fallen in with a group of super-powered superstars and felt more than a little afraid at how I was meant to fit in. *If* I was meant to fit in. Who knew how long they'd want me around?

"Does anyone else live here?" I asked, when the English language had returned to me.

"Just us. Service staff come and go. A cleaner and a gardener. Oh, and a cook, of course." Jake pulled his car up at the front steps and we all unloaded. His gorgeous sporty wheels looked right at home parked out the front of this place.

"Of course," I whispered.

Jake threw a duffle bag over his shoulder from the trunk

of the car and made an "after you" gesture with his other hand.

I took a tentative step toward the wide front doors. Emma grabbed my hand and dragged me at a run. "You're going to have the room next to mine. Come on, I'll show you around."

I get a room? For how long? Something felt twisted and defiant, deep down inside me, but this was obviously what I wanted. I *wanted* to be here, with other empaths, with Jake, with all of this magnificence. I was probably just hesitant because everything was happening so fast.

Emma's tour was informal at best. She dragged me fast-paced down wide halls that mostly looked the same to me, with walls painted stark white and floor-to-ceiling windows showing a view of the sea.

"Garage is downstairs that way. Living rooms and all the general stuff through there, but there's a second lounge area back that-away. Kitchen is 'round there; it's near my room, so that means it will be near your room! The boys' rooms are all off down that hall in the other wing." She pointed in vague directions. Even if she'd stopped and showed me each one, I was sure I'd get lost in there anyway.

"Whose place is this?" I asked.

"It's a serviced rental. We kind of move around a lot. I think Jake's planning another move soon."

"Oh?" I asked nonchalantly as my heart sank.

"Or he was before we picked you up." She grinned at me. "I hope we get to stay here a bit longer now. This is our best place yet."

"It must be so nice, travelling around, going on adventures, helping people." I cringed and smiled bashfully at Emma. "So, that sounded lame. But I won't lie — you guys are my new idols. How did you all get together?"

Emma twirled and started walking backward to look at me while she talked. "Jake and Jamie are brothers. You probably noticed."

I nodded and followed along after her. They had that brotherly vibe, as well as being like different-sized versions of each other.

"They've been doing this gig most of their lives. I guess the whole 'path thing runs in families sometimes, or whatever causes it can hit siblings or people growing up closely together. We don't really know what it's all about. We just know we have it and it's cool." Emma flicked her hair as if to emphasize the coolness.

I had to agree, but had hoped they'd have more info to share on this 'whole 'path thing.'

Emma kept talking. "So anyway, Jake and Jamie found

Donny first. None of us know much about Donny. He's the quiet type. But a good guy. That's when they realized there really were other people like them out there, outside their family, and made more of an effort to look. Wasn't long after that they found me. At a funeral, would you believe it?"

I wasn't sure what to say. Who had died? Were the deceased and Emma... close?

Emma kept smiling, despite the flash of grief and guilt coming from her. "Then it's been, like, forever, with just us. I've been wishing for another girl on the team. And here we are. Ta-da!" Emma swung a door open and gave me a nudge into the room with her hip. "Nice?"

I shook my head. Not nice. *Incredible*. There was a king-sized modern four-poster bed with billowy sheer white drapes. Wide-screen wall-mounted television. Doors to what I imagined were a walk-in-robe and en suite. Wide bay windows. Ocean view. A *balcony*. I panted a little.

"I know, right?" She grabbed my hand and gave it a squeeze, sharing in the excitement. "I told you you'd love it here. I called ahead and got Ms. Penny to set the room up for you while she was cleaning. You probably want a shower after being up all night. I know I do. There'll be towels in the bathroom, and you can borrow shampoo and stuff from my bathroom next door. Help yourself to whatever you like."

Emma opened the door and showed me the en suite. The other door was a walk-in closet, empty except for a bathrobe and slippers. I was suddenly conscious that I only had one set of clothes with me—the ones I was wearing.

I compared my average, straight-up-and-down figure to Emma, who was tall and impossibly curvy for her slim frame. She was dressed like a celebrity's supermodel girlfriend, in a tight leather skirt and deep-necked dress-shirt and high heels. I doubted she'd have much that would fit me, let alone suit me.

"I didn't pack," I muttered, dazed. I didn't do anything other than get on a plane without planning. I sat down hard on the bed, opposite the doorframe where a small white box was mounted. What was that? Where were the phones? I hadn't even told my parents where I was going. *What was I doing? I didn't think things through very well.* My skin turned clammy.

"Honey, we'll buy you whatever you need. You're special, like us; you can have whatever you want. And now I have a girl to go shopping with! We are going to buy you so much stuff." Emma came and sat next to me. She put her arm over my shoulder and squeezed. "You okay? Oh, you're probably coming down from the buzz. That would have been your first major use of the powers, right?"

"Is this what happens? I feel like I don't know anything yet. Do I need training or something?" I flopped back onto the bed, my feet still dangling over the edge.

"We don't really do the training thing. More like learn on the job. It mostly comes naturally anyway."

"So it just happens? Or do I need to make it happen?"

"A bit of both. Some of the power kicks in naturally, but you can focus to absorb even more." Emma lay back on the bed as well, propped up on one elbow. Her hair fell around her like a curtain and smelled of raspberries. "It's like when someone is feeling a strong emotion, it sort of floods out of them. Like the human mind—or heart, I don't know—can't hold so much feeling inside." She made her hand into a fist and placed it on her chest. "Ever felt like that? Like your emotions are more than you can stand? It's that excess we can tap into. I mean, emotions are powerful, right?"

I put a hand on my own chest, mirroring her. "When those looters came at me, I managed to protect myself, sort of. They were so angry and it was like their energy rushed into me, and I moved faster than I'd thought I could. And I should have bruises and cuts, but I don't."

Emma shifted down onto her back as well and punched her hands at the air above her. "It's bad ass, right? Hate sets up our bodies to fight, gives us strength and healing. Excitement gives us energy. Fear speeds us up. There's obviously a lot of overlap with emotions so it all gets a bit fuzzy."

"What about other emotions? Sadness?"

"Ick. Avoid sad people. Despair is just useless." Emma stuck her tongue out like she'd tasted expired milk.

"Love?"

"Aw, you're cute! I wouldn't go holding out to experience tapping into true love if I were you. Lust is where the power's at." She winked at me and I blushed.

Emma's pocket started pinging and she tugged out her phone from the skin-tight skirt. "It's Jake. Ooh, another job already?"

Wow. This place was so big, they texted each other inside.

"Come on. Let's go get the info." She grabbed me by the hand and we were off again. I was caught up in a red-headed whirlwind and her enthusiasm was contagious. I found myself giggling at how lost I was when we reached a lounge room lined with bookshelves where the guys waited.

The boys had showered, and somehow, they looked even more handsome than they had before. It made me self-conscious of the scent of overnight flight I wore. Jake had changed into a tight black tee under a leather motorbike jacket. I barely noticed the other two guys who stood either side of him. It was as though their hotness just enhanced Jake's. Side-kicks beside the most powerful superhero.

He smiled at me and I felt like I was in the right place again.

"What is it?" Emma bent at the knees and sprang up like an excited child.

"I'll tell you on the way. We have to leave right now if we're going to get anything done. Livvy, I'm sorry to do this to you, but we really can't miss this one. I'd bring you along, but it's too dangerous for someone so fresh."

My inner voice whined like a little puppy being left home alone. I didn't understand why they couldn't even tell me where they were going or what they were doing. Paranoia scratched at the corner of my brain. Jake patted me on the shoulder and all my worries floated away. *Don't be selfish, Livvy. They've just got important hero stuff to do.* "Yeah, I understand. Umm... what should I do?"

"Get settled in, cleaned up, relax. Ms. Penny left after her morning rounds but Sophie, our cook, is in, so feel free to call the kitchen on the intercom for whatever you need and she'll help you out." Jake pointed at an intercom near the door. I had seen one like it in my room too, but I hadn't known what it was at the time.

"Take a car into town if you like, or just hang here. We've got all the channels," Jamie added, and they headed to the door and down the hall.

Emma popped her head back in. "I'll take you shopping tomorrow, I promise!"

I nodded and remained planted in the room as their footsteps faded.

My first move was to inspect the intercom, and press the button labelled 'Kitchen'.

A husky woman's voice buzzed out of the box. "This is Sophie."

"Hi, um, I'm Livvy." I paused, embarrassed.

"Hi, love. What can I do for you?"

"I think I'm lost."

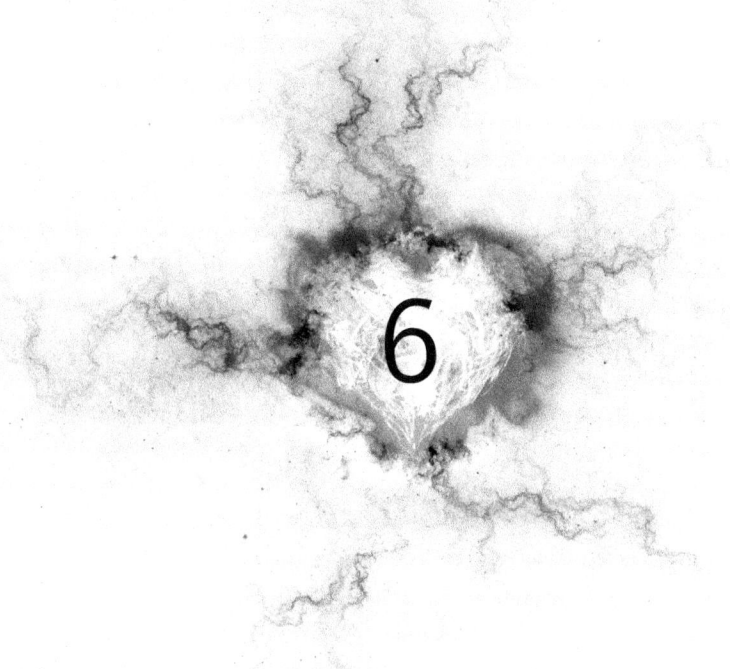

6

Sophie managed to find me from my description of the room in which I had been left, and gave me a slightly more formal tour than Emma's. The house layout was actually well structured and not nearly as daunting as I'd first believed. She made me a range of cute brunch-style snacks that looked like they were from a fancy restaurant and left me to explore.

It had been so good spending last night with them all. A bond had formed between us, and it was as if I really belonged. A secure contentedness had made me glow and want to stay with them forever.

Now I was on my own, hours from home. I felt like an

intruder here without the team. I kept feeling confused, concerned about how I'd ended up here and what I'd left behind. Like a pair of uninformed parents, and my phone charger. My phone lay lifeless on the bed.

The day was getting on. Even if Trevor had assumed I went home, or my parents had assumed I'd stayed longer at the shelter, sooner or later one would contact the other and there would be trouble. *What was I thinking? My parents must be freaking out.*

I attempted to turn on my phone, hoping for a last scrap of power, but it didn't respond, and there were no cables of the right kind in the house. Even Sophie had left her phone at home, and this palace seemed to be designed for room-to-room communication only with no visible landline. And with Jake off who knew where for who knew how long, getting home again was off the cards as well, for now. I felt stuck. Almost trapped.

I filled my stomach, took a shower, and put my dirty clothes back on, feeling apprehensive and, well... flat-out grouchy. Angry at myself for getting into this situation. Upset at being left alone.

To fill the time until the team returned, I decided to find the garage.

I never found it.

Instead, I stumbled across what had to be a prestige car showroom. When Jamie said to take a car, I didn't realize what sort of selection he meant. They had six cars between them, each of which probably cost as much as six ordinary cars, or, you know, a *house*. I barely recognized the badges, except ones like Maserati, and I only knew that one from TV shows about rich people.

I buzzed Sophie in the kitchen again and told her I'd be going for a walk. I didn't have a driver's license yet—thanks again to my parents' no-car policy—and even if I did, the stress of scratching up one of those cars could turn me prematurely gray.

But I did want to get out of that place. The big building left me at a loss without the others around, and I was never very keen on watching TV alone. On screen, I saw changes in the faces of the actors, but they lacked energy or the connection I felt in real life.

I figured I'd head into town and kill time at a cinema. While TV left me cold, I always loved going to the movies. I guess I understood why now. My empath abilities couldn't pick up emotions across a small screen, but they could pick up the vibe of a room of people sitting in the dark, all feeling the same thing.

Sophie asked if I'd be needing dinner. I still had twenty bucks cash on me, so I said I'd find something while I was out. I hoped I'd also find a pay phone. She gave me the visitor's security code for the keypad entry to get back in and I headed off. I felt almost surprised, and relieved, that I was allowed to leave. Was I being paranoid or what?

The mansion was at the top of a hill, and a long, winding road led down into town, past a few other mansion-like estates perched on the rocky cliff-side, overlooking the sea. A salty breeze from the ocean pushed at my back.

Sophie had given me directions to the cinema and it proved easy to find. I bought my ticket but was disappointed when I went in and was the only person there. It proved more depressing than watching TV.

By the time the movie was over, it had grown dark, and so had my mood. I found myself wandering aimlessly through the unfamiliar town, trying to get my thoughts in order. I questioned how long I'd been wandering but had no way to check the time. I'd made my way into an area where every second storefront was boarded up and layered in crude graffiti.

Despite the lofty elite on the hillside, the town looked like it had seen better days. It made my hometown look downright posh with its little boutique shops like Mom's.

Mom.

I swallowed hard. Mom and Dad must have been frantic.

I hadn't found a pay phone that hadn't been vandalized and was no longer functioning. I dreaded making the call to my parents even if I did have a way. I had no idea what I'd tell them, or how much trouble I'd be in.

I tried not to beat myself up too much. I'd just had some life-changing events take place. I was fine, and I'd let them know as soon as I could.

It was fine. They'd be fine. Everything was fine.

Who am I kidding? I went missing during a natural disaster. There was probably an amber alert out on me.

I've stuffed up big time when I really need my parents to be okay with this.

I needed to be able to tell them that my dreams were coming true and I had to follow them. Could they be okay with that? With me staying with the team? I would have been off to college in a year anyway... now I didn't even know if I was going back to school. I had no idea what was ahead of me, but it wasn't as though college had an Empath 101 course I could take. But still, how did working with these guys equate to money? Earning a living? Or would their trust fund look after me?

Shaking my head, I decided I needed to stick with Jake and the team. Regardless of anything else, I trusted Jake. One way or another, I felt that he'd look after me. It was why I was here, despite it seeming completely crazy.

While my mind did loop-de-loops trying to justify my actions, a sound caught my attention. A range of noises reminding me all too clearly of my confrontation with the looters—taunting, laughing, the sounds of anger and hard objects thudding against flesh.

It came from a side street up ahead.

My pace slowed. If someone was in trouble, maybe I could do something. It wouldn't be like last night. Surely I could use my powers properly, now I knew what they were.

I wasn't the old me anymore. Now, I was superhero princess me. Awesome Olivia was there to help.

I approached the side street carefully, going over the pros and cons in my head. No chance to call the cops this time. My flat phone had been left back in my room. If I did this, I'd have to do it with caution. I'd have to be clever. Jake hadn't mentioned secret identities yet and I didn't see the other guys wearing costumes, but I assumed it was best not to flaunt my powers.

I peeked around the corner.

Under a flickering street light, two guys were beating on a third. They had him pressed to a wall between them, taking turns slugging him in the stomach. They called him names—homo, trailer trash—disgusting, offensive names. The guy they beat didn't struggle and I worried they'd already done serious damage.

I tried to tap into their emotions, get some strength, speed, something I could use.

A cold emptiness crept over me instead.

Maybe I wasn't close enough? *Damn it, how did this work?* Their victim looked in a bad state and they showed no signs of slowing down. I had to do something fast.

Stepping into the alley, I took a position hidden in the shadows and yelled, "Police. Stop what you're doing."

All three jumped at my voice, and the emptiness cleared. A wave of anger, excitement and fear flowed off the attackers, and power built inside me. *Oh yes, I can do this.*

The two holding the third guy down blocked most of my view of him, but they all seemed about my age. The pair of bullies wore beanies, one blue, one red, probably from sports teams, but what would I know. My family was more likely to attend an art gallery opening than watch a football match. They muttered between themselves, then one of them called out, "You're no cop. Just get gone. You seen nothing here."

I flexed an arm, feeling the strength in it. I reveled in that power. Part of me wanted to use it, fly in like a superhero and show those bullies how it felt to get a beating. But I tried to stay smart. The power was my safety net only. Also, I really didn't want to nearly rip someone's hand off like I had last time. "Come on, guys, just leave him alone. I'm not going anywhere, and I don't think you want a witness here."

The beanie twins did that chin-lift thing guys do when communicating without words. One kept a hold of their prey and the other stalked toward me.

I took a step back out onto the main street to see if there was anyone else around, but it was empty. *Up to me then.*

I stepped forward and squared off against blue-beanie-boy. He twitched and swayed slightly. He had a badly grown goatee and up close, he stunk of alcohol.

"She's just some skinny chick!" he called back to his mate. He laughed and turned away. "Get lost!"

He spat out a swear word and headed back to his friend.

I followed at his heels. "I'm not going to let you keep beating that guy."

"Don't." The grunt of opposition came from the guy against the wall. He slouched, as though he'd fall if red-beanie-boy's hand on his shoulder didn't pin him in place. Stringy hair fell over his face. His effort to talk earned him another fist in the stomach.

"See? No one wants you around." Blue-beanie-boy spun back at me and thrust out an arm to push me away.

I sidestepped easily and he lost balance. His whole body fell forward after his arm and he landed hard on the pavement near the overflowing trash cans.

As he hit the ground I felt the force of his anger burst around him, accompanied by his loud swearing. I made an effort to absorb it all, like soaking in sunshine through my skin. My body responded, every cell working at perfect efficiency. I pulsed with strength.

He pushed himself back off the ground and dusted off his knees. "You're going to get it!"

He came at me swinging.

I maneuvered around a street sign and his fist cracked on the metal instead. More swearing. I had no problem keeping away from him, drunk and uncoordinated as he was, but I was only making him angrier. I wanted them to back off and leave without having to hurt anyone. Brilliantly, all I'd done was prove for a second time that me on my own wasn't intimidating enough to scare off angry guys.

After another bout of swearing, his friend let his victim go and came to join in. He didn't stumble around like drunken blue-beanie. The two of them advanced together. I stepped away, not wanting an all-in brawl. They backed me into a urine-scented corner of the alley. Their expressions were vicious. I lifted my fists, ready to fight back.

Down the street, a siren wailed. *Perfect timing.*

I shrugged innocently. "Did I forget to mention I *already* called the cops? Time to run, kiddies."

Their anger shed from them, replaced instantly with fear. After a quick glance at each other, and more swearing, they finally took my advice and bolted off into the night.

I took a few deep breaths and the siren passed by the other end of the alley, revealing the red of a fire truck. *Close one.* The bullies were well on their way though, and didn't notice my trick. It was over.

I just saved someone. All on my own. I let out a whoop and punched the air, grinning like a fool.

The guy they'd beaten had slumped down against the wall, his knees against his chest. He seemed to be catching his breath as well.

I held out my hand to help the guy up. "Are you okay?"

He ignored me and pushed himself to his feet with one shoulder against the wall. A breath hissed out through his clenched teeth. "What were you thinking? You shouldn't have gotten involved. You could have been hurt."

I froze with my hand still outstretched but my smile slipped right off my face. Not exactly the response I'd expected. "I...

I just wanted to help."

He turned and faced me fully. Average build, baggy clothing, dusty brown hair, pasty skin—nothing special at all. But his eyes transfixed me. Gray like wet concrete, they held me like a trap and the coldness I felt earlier crept back in.

"I didn't need your help. This happens all the time."

"A playful rumble, huh? What if they went too far?"

He just shrugged like he didn't even care. He winced as if each small movement hurt him, even talking. He was in pain but his face was blank, and I couldn't read a single emotion from him. It irritated me more than his criticisms of my rescue effort.

He glanced at me again with those eyes, looking me over as though checking for damage. "You were lucky they didn't mess you up."

"I wasn't lucky, I was…" I couldn't tell him what I really was, that I had superpowers. But even if I didn't. "I was clever, and capable, and I saved you!"

I found myself yelling. I couldn't read him at all and it threw me. *Why wasn't he happy I helped him? Happy to be saved?*

Blood dripped from his nose onto his light gray T-shirt. He zipped his jacket up over it and pulled the hood over his head. "Whatever."

He walked away.

All energy was drained from me. I spent my last cash to get a taxi back up to the mansion. I found it empty. Confused, frustrated, and alone, I crawled into bed.

I couldn't sleep. Gray eyes kept haunting me. Stupid, unappreciative eyes.

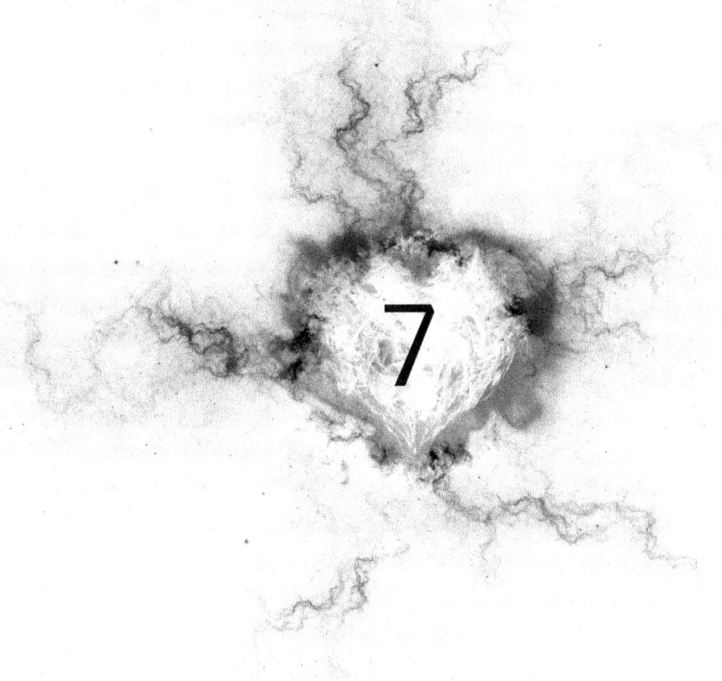

7

Jake and the team returned mid-morning. Seeing him again knocked my dull mood away. It also felt better having clean clothes. Ms. Penny had washed and dried what I'd been wearing while I had breakfast in bed in a robe and slippers. Pretty people and decadence took the edge off real quick.

We all sat in a lounge room. I wasn't sure which one or what its exact designation was, but a different one to yesterday. The white leather couches were immaculate and the rug so dense and fluffy, I almost wanted to sit on it more than the couch.

The guys relaxed from whatever their secret overnight mission had been, yawning and checking their phones amid a pile of empty energy drink cans and coffee mugs.

I didn't want to disturb them, but I had to deal with contacting my parents. I felt lame bringing it up, but none of that could match how upset my parents probably were.

I mustered up the will to speak. Jake smiled at me, and I almost lost it. Concentrating on something other than his perfect features proved difficult.

"Is there a way I can get my phone charged? I need to call my parents."

Jake sat next to me with his feet up on the glass coffee table and his head back. He straightened up to look at the powerless phone I exhibited in my hand. "Don't worry about it. We'll get you a new phone."

"Oh, I just need a charger, really. I don't need—"

"Ems, you taking our new girl out shopping today?" Jake spoke over me.

Emma had draped herself full-length down the opposite couch, leaving Donny and Jamie in designer egg-shaped armchairs, which looked more fancy than comfortable, at least for guys of their size.

Emma moaned and pouted, lifting her head with exaggerated effort. "Yeah, sure. I could probably stay awake for shopping. Let me chill out for a bit first though, K?"

The longer this waited, the more the knot in my stomach tightened. What would my parents be thinking? They probably thought I was buried under a collapsed building somewhere. "It's just, I really need to call my parents, like, yesterday. Maybe could I borrow someone's phone to let them know where I am?"

Jake shuffled across the lounge and put his arm around my shoulders.

The knot vanished. A warm glow replaced it and I tried not to purr.

"You're worried about your folks, about them worrying about you? I forget sometimes what that's like. Me and Jamie have been on our own for so long. Do you want me to take you home?"

He sounded so disappointed, like I was a child who'd had enough of a birthday party. Yesterday I might have said yes to leaving, but not now the team were all back here with me. I didn't want to be anywhere else. "Oh, no, I can just call them. I'm sure they'll be angry, but I need—"

Jake gave my shoulders a squeeze. "Do you want me to sort it out for you? Look, I'm great with parents, and it's always better to deal with things face-to-face, right? I've got to head back to your town tomorrow anyway, so I'll stop by and smooth things over. Save you from bearing the parental brunt."

I tilted my head and winced, working up to say no, which was hard. But seriously, my parents could have called me in as a missing person by now. I had to fix this.

Jake took my chin in his hand, leaning so close I almost thought he was going to kiss me. "Let me do this for you."

Warmth washed over me. I exhaled over wobbly lips. I smiled and gave my okay. My parents could wait another day if it meant getting an in-person explanation instead of dodgy phone call, and I just knew Jake could make them understand. He made everything better just by being there. He would explain everything, and everything would be okay. I could feel it.

"I could go with you, if you'd like. See my parents too and—"

"Livvy, we want you right here this week so at first sign of an event nearby we can take you with us. It's time to get to know you better and see how your powers manage," Donny said.

Emma sat up with far more energy than she'd shown before. She clapped her hands together. "Then you can be part of the team for real!"

I glowed, and wondered if it was visible to them all.

"What do you want me to tell your folks?" Jake asked.

I thought for a moment. "Tell them I'm following my dreams."

Emma did take me shopping that afternoon, but we didn't

get a new phone. We mostly bought new clothes for Emma. She held nothing back, snapping up every designer item taking her fancy, paying cash for everything. And everything wasn't cheap. She tried to encourage me to do the same, but I only managed to humbly request a new pair of jeans, two tops, some PJs and some underwear. At least I had some clothes to change into now. I was sure that soon I'd feel more comfortable taking what I wanted like Emma did.

Soon, I'd be part of the team for real.

During the week each of the team members ducked out individually for this or that. They weren't much for explaining what they were doing or where they were going, and I didn't want to seem naggy with my questions. Maybe they had day jobs? I somehow doubted it, unless it was just as cover for their secret identities. No way did they need the money.

No one did any empath power training, which disappointed me. There was so much I wanted to know, but they didn't even seem as interested in it as I did. The only training done was daily body-sculpting workouts. I joined in and they encouraged me, even though I was pathetic.

Jake returned from Bellscroft with a new phone for me, already programmed with the team's numbers, and a report on my parents.

"They were worried, of course, but my top-notch empath skills had them feeling better in no time. Here, check this out." Jake opened the photo gallery of the new phone and showed me a ten-second video of him sitting on my couch with my parents, all three smiling and waving.

"What did you tell them?" I had run through that discussion so often in my own head. Of course I wanted to be a good daughter and be honest, but the truth in this case was kind of wild, and not just my secret to keep.

"I told them we were friends from school, that we picked you up and let you stay at ours instead of the shelter. Made a few other excuses about flat phones, extra volunteer work together, following your dreams, yadda yadda, and they're happy to let you stay with us as long as you like."

I wondered if *forever* was included.

It felt sort of wrong to have not told them the whole truth, and there was something weird about seeing them so cheerful in that video. Was I upset that they weren't more worried? Maybe, but I was happy too. I needed to go back home myself for a visit sometime soon, and I reminded myself to give my parents super-hugs for letting me do this.

I knew Mom would understand. Mom ran away from a backwater slum when she was fourteen and lived on her own for years, waitressing in cafes during the days and working nights and weekends building her own business. She met the man of her dreams and now ran her own shop. My mom was amazing and always encouraged me to follow my dreams too. Not that I could compare my little adventure with what she'd done.

I thanked Jake for the new phone, and tried it out by taking a photo of us together. I spent most of my free hours for the rest of the week staring at that photo.

On Sunday night, Donny and Jamie called in from the industrial district across the city. A warehouse had gone up in flames. They said it looked like a good first event for me.

It was time for me to prove myself, although the idea of a whole burning building intimidated me. I'd never witnessed a real fire before. What would I be expected to do?

I felt too embarrassed to ask and appear dumb to the others. I just agreed to go.

This was my chance to use my powers as a part of the team.

Maybe I could save someone's life.

8

Jake drove the Maserati there faster than I thought was safe. Emma took the front seat and I squeezed into the pocket-sized back with Emma's reasoning that I had the shortest legs.

Maybe Jake sensed my anxiety, because he explained the situation more as we stopped down the road from the pillar of black smoke marking the fire.

"Don't stress. There's no one in the buildings. The whole industrial park has been evacuated. Nothing but stock and structures at risk." Ever the gentleman, he popped his front seat forward and helped extract me from the back of the two-door sports car.

I noticed Donny's black Jeep parked a little farther down the street. He and Jamie loaded something into the back. We wandered down to meet them.

"So, what will I be doing?" I tried to sound brave and eager.

Jake nodded to the other guys before coming back to my question. "Just watching. The firefighters are working hard to get the fire under control before it spreads. There's some serious adrenaline and emotion involved in that, so just feel out the situation and see what you can use. Then show us what you've got."

We were still a building or two away and I already felt the heat. I wondered if it was from the fire or the emotions of those fighting it. Or maybe just the warmth I always felt from being near Jake.

We ducked through a hole in a chain-link fence, sneaking closer between the warehouses. We found a viewpoint nearby and hid behind a stack of wooden pallets so the officials wouldn't send us away.

"What would you guys normally be doing, if I weren't learning?"

"For a fire? Not really a lot. Empath powers don't really make us more effective at putting out flames. We don't suddenly get super flame-retardant breath or anything. But If someone was inside, I'd rush in for the save, of course." Jake smiled and winked.

Could I rush into a burning building to save someone? Mouthing off at punks seemed altogether different to that level of heroism.

But I wanted to be someone who would do that. And I wanted to be *with* someone who would do that.

I stared happily at Jake for a moment too long before the fire drew my attention.

The two-story warehouse glowed like a jack-o'-lantern. I gaped in awe at such destructive, beautiful power. Flames painted the walls and the heat dried my unprotected skin even from this distance. The smell was off, like bad eggs and car burn-outs. Fortunately, most of the smoke blew the other way.

We watched the fire fighters doing their thing, calling orders back and forth, dragging hoses, working pumps on the truck. All knew their roles. They worked as a team. I'd be part of a team like that soon, but even better. I looked sidelong at Jake, his hair and skin glowing golden in the firelight. *Part of his team.*

Excess emotions flowed off the firefighters and I made myself a magnet, letting the power soak in through my pores.

Jake bumped my shoulder with his. "How are you feeling? Got the mojo yet?"

"Yeah, feeling good. Awesome even."

Jake held up his palm flat in front of me. "Give me your best shot."

"Really?"

Jake rolled his eyes. "And don't be holding back. We don't take wimps."

I raised my eyebrows and lifted my fist to the challenge. I could feel my muscles tense and coil. The sensation and awareness, the pure power, made me feel giddy.

I smacked my fist into his palm. The sound echoed like a log smashing the ground.

Jake whistled, shaking off the hurt dramatically. "Nice, some real potential there. Let's see how fast you are. How about a race?"

My imagination went on its own race into the future, Jake and me running through deserted warehouses, giggling, speeding after each other, tumbling into a heap, our lips so close and then...

Something caught my eye over at the fire.

My sight had improved as well, the way it had the night after I volunteered at the shelter. A sheet of corrugated iron peeled itself off the roof, lifting under the hot gusts from the fire like a strange kite. It lingered in the air then fell in a deadly dive bomb straight at one of the firefighters.

I ran.

I bolted toward the man. I'd never moved so fast. *Was I still visible or just a blur?*

I collided with the firefighter in a tackle and we rolled six feet, tumbling together. The corrugated iron scraped and tore on the concrete right where he had been.

The firefighter looked from me to the jagged, red-hot iron and back again with his jaw unhinged. His face softened and I held my breath, waiting for the praise I'd missed with the last save I made.

Instead I found myself wrenched to my feet and dragged away.

"Idiot! What were you thinking?" Jake hissed as he pulled me along, jostling me roughly as I stumbled to keep up. We moved fast and were back at the car before I knew it. "We can't be seen here. You can't do things like that! People will start asking questions."

I stuttered, screwing my face up to stop myself crying. He might as well have slapped me. "I... I didn't do good?"

"It's important we all keep a low profile." Jake's eyes had turned stony. "You're not going to be trouble for us? Trying to be a big hero?"

"No, I..." I had been trying to be a hero. Was that wrong?

I felt like a dumb, naïve child to have thought saving a life in the real world would be like it was on TV. Everything had repercussions and I had acted without considering any consequences for myself or Jake's team. I hung my head. "I just wanted to help him. I'm sorry. I get we have to do things carefully."

Emma, Jamie and Donny caught up. I looked around them for support but could tell they were all irritated, or downright angry. I felt broken inside, and tried to wipe away a tear before the others saw it on my cheek.

Jake softened and my world turned right again. "It's okay. It's easy to get caught up in the power sometimes. You did a good thing. Just remember, if you're going to be part of the team, you have to learn to take orders. No running off and being a hero on your own."

I nodded, relieved as the team's anger at me lessened. "Of course. I can do that. I'll follow orders. I want to be part of the team more than anything."

No one talked on the drive home. I kept busy berating myself internally. I had to be smarter or they wouldn't accept me. I should have known I wasn't special enough as is to get an easy A on their empath tests. I never was good at exams.

Those thoughts mixed with the thrill I'd felt when saving the fireman's life. Even if it was wrong to expose myself or my powers, deep inside I felt like I'd done the right thing. Jake was probably just angry I got there first and beat him at his own hero game. Maybe he was secretly impressed.

Would the fireman have thanked me if he'd had the chance?

Of course he would have. Only emotionless gray-eyed robot types didn't thank people.

Once those eyes came into my head, I couldn't wipe them away again for the rest of the night.

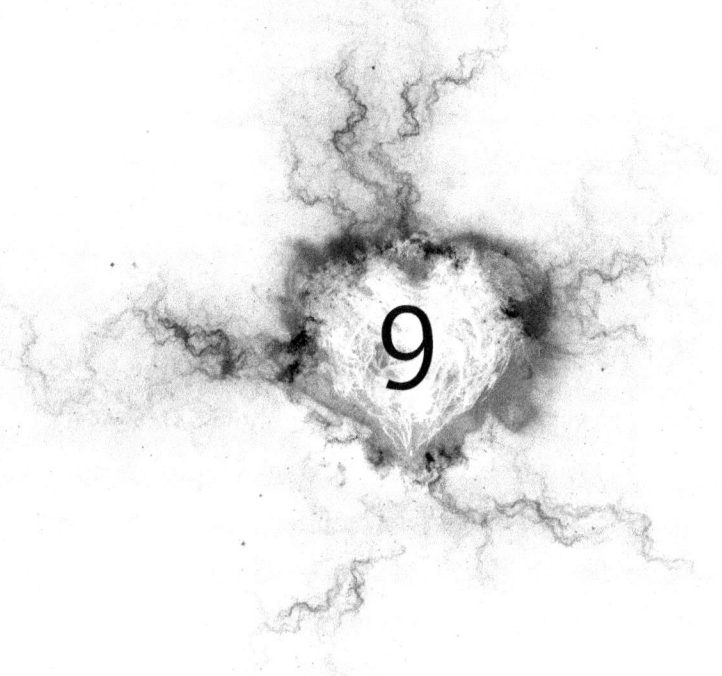

9

woke up the next morning to Emma jumping on the side of my bed. I gasped, shocked out of sleepiness by her sudden appearance in my room.

She giggled and headed back out the door, calling over her shoulder. "Come on, get up. Make yourself pretty and meet us in the formal lounge. We'll be waaaaaiting."

Could it be? Formal lounge, formal initiation into the team?

I rushed through a shower and put on my best choice of limited clothing. I tried three options for my hair then left it out long, running Emma's straightener over just the front to tidy it up.

I tried two lounge rooms before I found the formal one

where everyone waited. I wasn't sure I'd been in this one before. A massive gilt-framed mirror dominated one wall, and everyone sat in armchairs around a stool in front of it.

Emma stood up, squealing. "It's makeover time!"

She ushered me onto the stool and I sat awkwardly, feeling like the star of a very terrible one-woman show. "Makeover?" I didn't see any wardrobe or makeup or hairdressing stuff.

Jake leant forward in his armchair and smirked, his wide shoulders on display in a fitted shirt. "We want you on the team, Livvy."

He wants me on the team. I didn't screw up. I beamed.

Jake continued, "So we need you to be the best you can be."

"Be. Yourself. But. Better!" Emma shouted, punctuating each word with a clap.

Okay, and that meant makeover? Could be fun. Just like on reality shows. I could go a fancy new hairstyle for sure. The prospect of dying it something other than brown had me smiling. I was getting the princess treatment again, and I liked it.

I had worried I'd blown it last night with my hero stunt. Jake didn't seem angry anymore, but eyed me critically, running a hand through his golden hair and rubbing his chiseled chin.

I tried to sit tall and not be overwhelmed with self-consciousness as everyone visibly judged my appearance. It was the hardest thing I'd done since *ever*.

Emma circled me and played with my hair. "You're already so pretty; there won't be too much work to do. Just need a few things to really make you pop."

I burned with a blush. People had told me I was pretty before, but I'd figured I was average-pretty at best. And *pretty* wasn't *amazing. It would be nice to be amazing like everyone else in this room.*

"If you have suggestions for my hair, I'm up for anything." I poked my loose hair to highlight my fashion cluelessness.

"We'll do the hair for sure, and much more. Don't worry. Any work you have done is on us." Emma grinned.

Hang on, what? "Work done?" I asked.

Jamie spoke up. "She should get her lips and tits filled."

I laughed out loud but no one else did.

My laughter shut off fast. "Oh. I thought you were joking."

Jake cut in with a soft tone. "Sorry, Jamie can be a bit crass. Don't worry; it wouldn't be that extreme. Not as much as Emma's had done. It wouldn't suit your frame."

Emma folded her arms under her abundant bust as though to demonstrate.

"She could also have the bridge of her nose taken down a little, and narrowed at the base," Donny said in his quiet, authoritative voice.

Jake nodded. "You're right, Donny. Always with the eye for detail."

I wanted to hide. Were they seriously talking about cosmetic surgery? Sitting there deciding on how to rebuild my body? They were pranking; they must have been. Just pushing it to see how long they could keep me going.

At least Jake wasn't joining in being as critical as the others.

"She needs to get some dental work done too. The crooked front teeth have to go," Jake said.

Something shattered inside me.

There was no joke here.

My mouth fell open as the concept settled in. *They expect me to get cosmetic surgery to be part of the team. And dental work.* I closed my mouth. Did I really think someone like Jake could be attracted to me as I was? Maybe not, but I'd hoped. I'd hoped he'd seen beyond the brown-haired, brown-eyed, average-pretty to something special inside. That had been my dream. Not him wanting to change me into something else.

"Honey, don't feel bad! It's not like it's just you. We've all had work done." Emma hugged me around the shoulders then pounced back into an empty armchair. "We're talking about way less for you than I had. But then, I wanted a lot of it myself."

All of them? Even the guys? I looked around at them, all like fresh-out-of-the-box action figures, and they suddenly seemed too perfect. All of them had been carefully designed and crafted. "Why?"

"To be this fab-u-lous," Emma drawled, posing like a model in her chair.

Jake tilted his head and gave me a kind smile. It helped settle my nerves better than hot chocolate. His smile made everything better and I started wondering if I could get plastic surgery, for him, if it would keep him near me, so I could always feel this warm and safe. "We all do it because it helps with our powers. Same with keeping ourselves in good shape. It pays off to be attractive."

"I told you. Lust is where the power is at," Emma said.

I frowned. "I don't understand."

Donny's voice was dryer than usual. He spoke slowly, like he was trying to wake a sleepwalker, or talking to someone really dumb. "When people are physically attracted to us, we receive power from that emotion. It means we can get them to do what we want. Anything we suggest is accepted easily, a bit like hypnotism. The more attracted they are, the better it works. So we make ourselves physically desirable. Did you really think we were all born this perfect?"

Emma chimed in. "Haven't you ever had it easy picking up guys and getting them to do whatever you want? Buy you drinks, give you their number, give you their whole damn wallet?"

Not really. There had never been anyone I was interested enough in to try picking up. I was waiting for my prince, my Jake. Sure, there had been a couple of guys who had hit on me before but I'd never thought that I could use that to my advantage, and why would I ask for their wallet?

Just how open to suggestion did this attraction power make people?

The air rushed out of me so quickly I felt faint. Would that power make someone open to the suggestion of leaving home with a group of strangers in the middle of the night?

Everything spiraled. *It can't be...* I stared at the floor, trying to take steady breaths.

I should have asked more questions. I should have gone home and thought about what I was doing. I should have asked my parents. Any sane person would have done those things. I liked to think I was, but I also didn't like the idea that Jake had used his powers on me. The two concepts couldn't co-exist.

I looked up to ask something, anything to get the reassurance that he hadn't done what I thought.

Jake smiled. His perfect smile. My concerns fell away like

sand under a wave. In the past, that wave buoyed me and left me floating blissfully, but now the water was cold, leaving me feeling numb and confused. Was it happening again? I could hardly tell my own desires and emotions over what I was being told I should do. *I do want this. I'm following my dream.* Maybe body alteration didn't fit into my dream but I hadn't ever been really clear on what my dreams were anyway.

"So, my lovely Livvy, the question is—what are you willing to do to be part of the team? If you can't even handle some cosmetic surgery…"

The thought that my chance to be part of the team was slipping away made me panicky. I didn't think I could cope with going home, being normal again after seeing how Jake and the others lived. The way I felt after saving the guy in the alley, after saving the fireman—maybe that was the dream I should be chasing. If I wanted to be a hero, to be exceptional, my best chance to do that was with these people who were unlike anyone I'd ever met before.

"Anything." I took a moment, my smile wide. This was the right decision. "I'll do anything."

10

I moped up and down the shopping mall, arms loaded with fancy bags from deluxe boutiques.

I should have felt like a celebrity, out on a spending spree with a fat wad of someone else's cash, but I was stressing about buying the right things to make myself look better. Like if I bought the right dress, the team would decide I looked fine just the way I was. Even if that could work, how was I supposed to know which dress that was? I was no style expert. I wished Emma was here to guide me, but she had gone off on some important lunch date. She had great fashion sense and everything she wore looked perfect on her, like it had been custom fitted.

Or was it her that had been custom fitted to the clothes? Just how much work had she had done to look so magazine-cover perfect? How did she look before?

After the 'makeover' meeting, Jake said he wouldn't rush me into anything major. It was all just something to think about for now. They wanted me on the team and seemed happy I was willing to do what I needed to be with them.

Jake told me there were so few people like us. Maybe he felt they couldn't leave me out, that they needed every empath they could find. But I had to step up and be valuable to the group. I had to be the best version of me, to fit in with them. *I just hope I can do it without going under the knife.*

Whether it was my thoughts or the swag weighing me down, I felt exhausted. I needed fuel, and stepped out of the glittery mall onto the street to find a coffee shop.

That was when I saw him again.

He sat across the street in a park. His eyes were down, reading a book, but I didn't need to see them to know their exact shade of gray.

I felt bad that I'd yelled at him. Sure, I'd saved him from further beating, and that was a point to me, but yelling at the victim wasn't very heroic behavior.

I decided to apologize and see how he was recovering. Now

we were in a less stressed environment, maybe he'd also say thank you, which I had to admit I really wanted. It wasn't just a validation thing. I needed reassurance to know I'd done the right thing, since "the right thing" was starting to get very fuzzy in my mind.

I took a deep breath to build up some courage and marched across the road.

Very few people were in the park, and if they were, they rushed through it like a shortcut rather than lingering in the neglected space. The swing set was rusted and both swings had been tangled up around the top beam. A wooden play fort dominated the central area. It was the kind which wouldn't get built these days for being too dangerous for kids, but the kind kids loved. A maze of timber rooms and too-high balance beams and splintery surfaces—it looked like adventure. One boy pointed longingly in its direction before being dragged the other way by his dad. The lawn throughout was uneven, spotted with dandelions and longer than it should be.

I shuffled through it to the bench where the guy I'd saved sat.

I stood still in front of him, and he didn't move.

Whether he was ignoring me, or absorbed in the dog-eared paperback, I couldn't tell. The same weird, cold, emptiness I'd felt when I first saw him crept into my bones. I cleared my throat and he looked up.

He looked better in the daylight, less pasty and more ivory skinned. I spaced out for a moment, wondering how my olive skin would look pressed against it. *Where did that thought come from?*

"Hi?" He sounded confused. Did he recognize me? I was wearing the same red trench coat I'd been wearing since leaving home, which I figured was pretty memorable.

There was a slight rosiness to his cheeks and under his eyes, almost like he'd been crying, but I couldn't get an emotional read on him.

"Do you remember the other night? I was, uh, in the alley, and those guys, and, um, I'm Livvy." My inability to sense any hint of emotion from this guy threw me. It was just like watching TV. I saw the movement and angles of his face and body but couldn't sense anything real. Almost as though he wasn't even really there.

"I remember." He nodded slowly. I wanted to face palm. Of course he remembered. It wasn't the sort of thing you'd just forget, like what you had for lunch last week. I shuffled on the spot, ready to leave in embarrassment.

"I'm Dean," he said, and a tiny smile emerged. Or maybe it was a nervous tic. I couldn't tell either way with this blank slate. Even Donny showed mountains of emotion in comparison. But that tiny smile gave me courage.

"I was just about to get a coffee. Want to join me?" I thumb-pointed over my shoulder at the café in front of the mall.

Dean stared at it for a moment, then back up at me, his eyebrows twitching. He closed his book. It was so worn, it had no real cover anymore. I wondered what he was reading.

"Sure."

He stood up and I juggled my bags back into carrying order as we crossed the road.

I paid at the counter for a cappuccino with extra froth and Dean waved off getting anything, just helped himself to some table water. We took a booth and my bags piled around me on the bench.

"So..." I struggled to be casual. "Are you feeling okay? Since, you know, I saved you from those guys?"

Dean shrugged and nodded but didn't say anything.

The red around Dean's eyes made them look less gray, more the color of worn denim. They had a depth I kept falling into, like a deep, icy lake. I couldn't help staring, trying to get some hint of what this guy felt. But all I got from him was that same chilling, hollow feeling.

He leaned back in the booth and unzipped his jacket. The

baggy shirt underneath was gray and it struck me that he seemed to be wearing the same clothes I'd seen him in before. Not that they were unique in any way to tell for sure. They were clean, and I smelled plain soap and a smoky musk as he took off his jacket. The stitching had come undone around the collar of the T-shirt and the fabric looked thin.

His hair fell in front of his face, feathery and also clean. Maybe it just looked stringy the other night from sweat.

His lips moved.

Shoot. I had completely missed what he'd said. "Uh, sorry, what?"

"I asked if there was something specific you wanted to talk to me about." When I hesitated, feeling foolish for the whole situation, he continued. "Are you okay? You seem upset. At least, you aren't smiling like a fool like you were after chasing off those guys."

Great. I had no idea what he was feeling and here he was making guesses about me.

I pulled my lips closed tight. "It's just my teeth. They're all crooked. I didn't mind so much before, but now I kind of hate them."

"You're prettier when you aren't doubting yourself."

He said it so plainly, like it was nothing. Not praise, not

flattery or a shot at getting something from me. He said it just like a fact, like *the sky is blue*.

Nothing Dean said felt like it had any emotion so I clung to his words for meaning. Like how he said *prettier* and that maybe the "er" meant he thought I was pretty even now when I was doubting myself. My heart was doing silly maneuvers and I shook my head, looked into my foamy coffee and added another sugar.

"Your teeth give you character. It's cute, the way one crosses over the other a bit at the front—"

I put my hand over my mouth.

"Sorry, I'm saying dumb things. But you shouldn't feel bad about them. I suppose you're going to get them fixed though, aren't you?"

I shrugged, not entirely sure if it was up to me.

"I guess you've got the money to get whatever smile you want." Dean eyed the bags surrounding me.

"Oh, the shopping. I kind of came to stay with friends for a while without packing and needed some things. The money isn't mine. It's sort of complicated." I shuffled around on the seat as though it would hide some of the mountain of purchases behind me, suddenly embarrassed by it all.

"What about that necklace? You were wearing it the other

night too. Silver, or...?"

"White gold." I wrapped my hand around the heart-shaped pendant I had been wearing since the earthquake, covering it from sight. "My parents bought it for me when I got a B on my last tests."

"Shouldn't that have been an A?"

"Probably, but B was the best I could do. It's not like I don't try; I just suck at tests." *And my parents are big softies.* My vision glazed with tears. I missed them so much. I blinked the wetness away.

Dean rolled his eyes. I didn't have to sense emotions to know the blatantly sarcastic 'poor you' look.

Did he think I was spoiled? Was that what he was getting at? This whole conversation had been weird. He was all questions and no answers. I wanted desperately to know why his eyes were red, whether he had been crying or not. Whether he had any feelings at all. I wanted to know how he felt about being attacked and how he felt about me saving him, and I couldn't read a thing.

Embarrassment unfurled inside me without warning, coloring my face. I gulped my coffee to hide it. Dean stared.

A beeping noise distracted me, and it took a moment to recognize the message tone of my new phone. I apologized and pulled it out of my pocket.

A message from Jake. I smiled at seeing his name, then pulled my lips back over my teeth again.

Coming to pick U up. Meet west mall exit. C U in 15. Team stuff.

I typed quickly. *Cya soon.*

I slipped the phone away and told Dean I had to be somewhere.

He helped me load my bags up again and thanked me for the coffee, even though he didn't have anything.

We stood for a moment, facing each other silently.

I wasn't sure if I'd see Dean again after this and I kind of wanted to. In the whirlwind my life had become, the last twenty minutes had felt like the only time recently when my feet were safely on the ground. There was something cooling, calming, and down to earth about Dean. Also something frustrating and confusing, but that just made me want to work him out even more.

I could ask for his number, but then what? He didn't seem that interested in me. He probably only came over for coffee to be polite. I should have just said goodbye, but instead I blurted out more crazy words. "You really think my teeth are okay?"

Dean half-smiled and walked away.

11

Donny's jeep screeched to a stop in front of me where I waited on the curb, doing a balancing act with my purchases. I threw them all in the back and climbed in next to Emma who shuffled into the middle seat. It was a full house, with Donny driving, Jamie shotgun, and Jake and I in the back with Emma as an unfortunate barrier between us. I handed the remaining unspent cash to Jake, and he pocketed it.

"So, team stuff?" I asked, hoping it was fun, heroic team stuff and not 'let's all point out Livvy's flaws' team stuff.

"Last night at the fire we were getting to know the strength of your powers. This afternoon, it's time to prove you're one of us, part of the team." Jake gave me a serious look, with just enough flirty smile to make me swoon. "We're doing a fundraising activity."

"Oh, like, charity work?"

Emma barked a high-pitched laugh that faded into a giggle. I frowned. *Since when is charity work funny?*

"Fundraising for us, for the team," Jake continued. "We're headed to a bank to make a withdrawal. We need to stock up on the spending cash."

Donny drove us downtown. The glitzy mall area made way for the industrial and housing estate district.

I shook my head. *They're just going to the bank? Why did this need to be done as a team?* Unease gurgled in my stomach. My paranoia grew sharp claws but I still refused to let it scratch down my perfect painted world.

Emma fished around in a massive designer handbag on her lap and threw what looked like a dead animal to Jamie. She grabbed more hair from the bag—wigs —and passed a black one to Jake. She took a blond wig in each hand and dangled them in front of me. "We're both going to be blond, like sisters! You're going to look so cute."

I took the wig with numb fingers. A buzz of excitement came from everyone else in the car. "We're not really withdrawing money, are we?" I wasn't sure I wanted to hear the answer.

"Sure we are," said Jamie. "Just not ours."

"Um…" That was the answer I hadn't wanted to hear.

Jake sighed, shaking his head. "My little brother and his abundant tact. Don't freak out. It's not a big deal. This is an easy job. Breeze in, breeze out. You're with us on this, aren't you, Livvy?"

"Um…" I hesitated again.

"We have to do this to stay a team. Do you think we should have normal jobs with our powers? We're better than that."

Donny glanced at me in the rear-vision mirror. "Taking on a new member is expensive too. Got to earn that back. Where did you think the money you spent today came from?"

Trust funds? Inheritance? Lottery winnings? That was all a bit naïve to assume. This was the real world, not one of my fantasies, even if it had felt like a dream come true. Did I really expect to just take and spend their cash with no strings attached? I'd gone out and spent their money, like I'd had every right. I'd put myself into debt with them. I shivered cold sweats.

"Are you really talking about robbing a bank here? That's all kinds of dangerous, and, well, illegal." My heart pumped hard and I wasn't sure what to think. It was all just too surreal. This was only-happens-in-movies stuff, not just-left-the-mall stuff.

"Honey, it won't be dangerous at all. We have superpowers, remember? We're just going to walk in, bat our eyelashes, ask for the money, and walk out with it. We already scoped this bank, and it's old school. No security screens or anything." Emma tugged her wig into place and reached between the front seats to adjust the rear-view mirror to preen. She then turned her preening onto Jamie and Jake's wigs, also now in place. They looked so different, their hair now jet black with mature cuts. It made them seem darker, more dangerous, somehow. "My lunch date was with a worker from there who told me all about the place. We would have left it a bit longer, but now's the best time to hit them. It's welfare check day, and the bank tops up its tellers for everyone coming in to cash their checks. Easy pickings."

Jake brushed Emma away and put on dark sunglasses. "Livvy, you're just going to be lookout for us this time. Until you get some work done, we won't have you taking on a teller, just in case."

I breathed out very slowly, letting the air puff out my lips. "I don't know if I can do this. Isn't it wrong?"

"No one will get hurt and the bank won't miss a few cash drawers. We're not taking the vault or anything insane. And we'll use the money to help us do more heroic stuff later on.

Promise." Jake winked, and I swore I heard Jamie chuckle.

Jake looked me in the eyes and I felt him forcing the sense of trust, warmth and contentedness on me. I pushed it away. It was easier now. With Jake's recent words and actions, I wasn't as attracted to him as I had been before. I saw clearly, felt clearly, and the horror of it almost overwhelmed me.

A physical pain crept into my chest. I was scared of Jake. Scared of what I was doing. Terrified of all of them and what they would do if I didn't cooperate. I had visions of jumping out of the moving car and trying to run away, but these guys had had use of their powers for longer than me. I was going to guess they'd be much faster than I was.

Jake watched me, waiting for my response. I felt trapped, but I couldn't let him see that.

I put the wig on and smiled. I read once just the act of moving your muscles into a smile made you happy and hoped it would be enough to cover my fear. I tried to shut off the part of my brain saying *no, no, no, no, no,* and focused on Jake's smile. It didn't help. *That fake smile.* How much of him was real at all? Everything felt wrong.

Emma tilted her head at me and giggled. "Donny, drive around the block a couple of times while I sort out this girl's hair."

12

Donny waited with the car down the street and Emma and I walked into the bank first.

It was a reasonably large place, old-fashioned, like she'd said, standing in a row of mostly closed shopfronts in a dying business district. Only a pawn shop, second-hand clothing store and tobacco shop were still open nearby.

Inside the bank, a musty smell rose from the threadbare carpet, and the wooden counters looked more like something out of an old western movie than a modern bank. Plexiglas dividers had been bolted on top of them, and a ticket machine stood at the entrance like a welcoming robot, but they were the only parts of the place that felt like they weren't from the 1950s. Even the customers were old, mixed in with a few younger tradesmen and laborers.

I was in a bank. About to rob a bank.

We were seriously going to rob a bank.

I played through my memories of how I'd ended up here, as though this were a pick-your-own-adventure book and I could just flip back to the right point and avoid this outcome.

So much of the time since the earthquake was a blur; I'd been hypnotized by these perfect people. *Perfect criminals*, I realized. But I couldn't only blame them. I'd made my decisions. I had wanted this.

Well, not *this*, exactly.

I made sure my oversized sunglasses were still in place and tugged down my wig as though I could cover all of my face with it. *If I just get through this, there has to be a way I can back out gracefully from this whole team thing, right? Will Jake just let me go?*

Emma scoped a security guard and went to do her job, flirting with him and keeping him entirely occupied. I just had to take a seat and keep watch. Only the bank was busy, and there were no seats left. Small detail, but I had to breathe through an anxiety attack as I tried to stand casually in the corner.

Jake and Jamie came in not long after us and took numbers from the machine. I practically counted the seconds waiting for them to be called to a teller, sure we were all about to be arrested at any second. I felt so thoroughly guilty, I was sure it could be seen oozing from my pores. I considered just flat-out bolting, but Donny was watching the street.

Jake was called, and Jamie a split second after as two tellers cleared. They were middle-aged ladies who I could tell were already swooning at the boys' approach. Maybe this would be easy after all.

I watched with fascination as Jake leaned forward, his lips almost up against the Plexiglas barrier. I saw the attraction radiating from the lady. She probably would have played with her hair if it weren't back in a very tight business-like bun. She kept on talking and giggling with Jake as she pulled a cash bag from the desk and opened the cash drawer, stuffing bills into the bag one wad at a time. No alarms went off. No one seemed to think anything suspicious was happening. It was business as usual and a bag of free cash for the team. I didn't like it. It felt so wrong. But I just wanted it to be over so I could breathe again.

Coldness crept across my skin.

I hoped it just meant the air-con had kicked in, but this felt familiar.

92

I'd felt this sort of chill before.

The teller with Jake froze, and her flirty grin dropped into a frown. She looked at the bag in her hand like she'd discovered she held a dead fish. I couldn't hear what she said, but her jaw wobbled up and down. I couldn't tell how she was feeling either; my empath senses had turned off. Jake kept working his act but she wouldn't calm down for him.

Jamie called over to Jake. He was having trouble too.

Jake called back, loud enough for me and Emma to hear, "Change of plans."

The teller stood and made to move away, and suddenly Jake had a shiny silver handgun pointed at her.

No, no, no, no, *no*.

Jamie pulled a gun from his jacket too, waving it at the waiting customers. "Everyone get back against that wall. You know the deal. If nothing stupid happens, then nothing stupid happens."

A large man in grease-covered clothing didn't budge. He drawled in a husky voice, "Come now, boys. Don't do anything rash."

"Stupid." Jamie dropped his aim and shot the man in the leg. He crumpled, gasping, clutching at the wound, trying to hold in his blood.

I yelped, my heart hammering. Jake shook his head at me, warning me with his expression. Others in the crowd screamed as well, cowering back.

I turned to Emma, just a few steps away from me with the guard. She couldn't be in on this. Not *this*.

She held a petite pistol in one hand and she relieved the security guard of his weapons with the other.

"Ems?" I hissed.

"Chill, sister," she hissed back. "A little firearm action will get the sheep scared and our powers kicking in again. Then we can get our goods and clear out fast."

But my powers weren't kicking in.

I didn't feel anything, not the slightest tingle, only the cold inside. People shuffled toward the wall, mumbling outrage and prayers. I looked over their faces, all of them terrified.

Except one.

His face was blank and his gray eyes stared at me, at my heart pendant, at the same clothing he'd seen me in just half an hour before and my disguise, the blond wig.

Dean.

I looked away, ashamed.

"I'm still not getting the vibe!" Jamie yelled at Jake, who was busy getting the teller to keep clearing drawers.

"Swap," Jake called back, and Jamie swung his gun to the teller, taking over.

Jake scanned the room, coming to stand beside me. "You feeling anything?"

"Just… cold." My eyes turned toward Dean automatically, just for a second too long. Jake's gaze followed mine and he grunted.

"A blocker. We've got a blocker!" Jake yelled to the others.

"Oh shit," Emma spat.

The hostages against the wall cowered. Dean stood motionless and continued to stare right at me.

Jake patted me on the shoulder. "Good pick, lookout. We'd be in trouble if you hadn't spotted him. You're making yourself valuable."

I didn't want to be valuable like this. I didn't understand much of what was happening and liked even less. "Why? What's a blocker?"

"People who shut away their feelings so hard it breaks something inside them. They mess with our powers," Jake ranted. "Best to deal with them when they show up. I've seen one block off an empath's powers for good."

Jake aimed his gun at Dean and smiled his comforting smile at me. That smile chilled me more than the blocking coldness coming from Dean. "Don't worry. Once we get rid of him, our powers will work again and we can get all this under control."

"Get rid of? What? No!"

I stepped in front of Jake to try and talk him out of it.

Jake swore and jerked the gun to the side.

Sound exploded through my skull. Everything went numb. My ears rang.

It took a moment to hear the screams behind me, to feel the burn in my cheek. My over-sized sunglasses hit the floor.

I turned in slow motion and saw an elderly woman falling to the ground. The pool of blood around her made acid rise in my throat. I knew she was dead, just knew it.

Other customers cried and ran.

Jake had lost control of the situation. People stumbled right over the old woman's body, stampeding toward the door. Emma and Jamie headed for the door as well. Sirens wailed in the distance.

Dean dodged between the crowd but didn't make for the exit.

"Run, get out of here!" I screamed at him.

He kept coming my way.

I felt hard, hot metal press against my temple.

"Jake?" I whimpered. I wanted to be strong, but it turned out a gun at your head could cause whimpering.

"I should have known you wouldn't work out, but I didn't think you'd screw things up this much!" he yelled at me, so close spittle hit my face.

His finger on the trigger tensed.

The gun fired. A body slammed against my side, pushing me away.

Dean cried out as he fell past me and hit the floor. Blood flooded through the fabric of his hoodie sleeve.

The coldness faded. I felt some power come back to me, like it had when I'd surprised Dean and his attackers that night. I guessed when he was shocked, he wasn't keeping his feelings under such tight rein and his emotional block didn't extend out. Or something. I didn't know. I just knew I had to act fast before Jake felt his powers kick in again too.

I had stumbled when Dean pushed me clear of the gunshot but I regained my balance fast. I spun with the momentum and knocked the gun from Jake's hand. I continued the spin and cracked my elbow against Jake's jaw, making him fall backwards.

I grabbed Dean by the arm, pulling him to his feet, practically threw him over my shoulder, and made a run for it.

13

I raced down empty alleys and side streets. Sirens blared around me, and I changed direction to avoid them. I was sure Jake was right on my heels, sure I would hear a gunshot go off again and that would be the end.

Dean bounced where I had him slung in a fireman's carry over my shoulder. Blood from his arm ran slick and warm down over my coat and onto the crisp white of my peasant blouse, the cutest of three tops I had chosen from to wear this morning to be judged by those... *bad guys*. How had we gone from makeover planning session to gunfight in just one day?

I hoped the jostling didn't hurt Dean too much, but I couldn't slow down. He was still out of it, which I guessed was the only reason I could keep moving at superspeed, could support his weight so easily. I couldn't risk being caught, but I had no idea where I was going or what I should do. I needed to help the guy who'd just been shot saving me. I only remembered one thing from first-aid class that seemed relevant: the DR ABCs. I had to get Dean and myself out of Danger then check his Responsiveness. That meant I had to get us as far away from Jake as I could. Airway, Breathing and CPR… *it better not come to that.*

Dean moaned and coughed and for a split second I felt relieved.

Then the coldness sank into me, leaching all my strength.

My legs buckled and we both hit the cracked concrete footpath. My knees grazed through denim as Dean's weight on my back crushed me forward.

I tried to roll him to the side without hurting either of us more. He moved off me, and leaned up against one of the graffiti-covered high metal fences enclosing the backyards around us.

His upper arm still oozed blood.

He opened those gray eyes and stared at me.

I blushed red all over. I had no idea what he thought of me right now. This was all my fault.

"We should get you to a doctor, or a hospital. We have to do something about your arm."

He turned his head to the gunshot wound, staring at it for a moment, expressionless. He brought his other hand up to suppress the bleeding. "No. Hate hospitals." He flinched at his own touch and stared at me again. "I don't understand you."

I coughed a hysterical laugh but only a breathy noise came out.

"Were you with *them*? Or are you just wearing a wig for fun?"

Reaching up, I patted the side of my head, feeling the curling blond waves of the wig. I tugged it off and dropped it on the weed-covered pathway.

"It's complicated." I didn't know how to explain without sounding bad, because there wasn't a way. I'd done the wrong thing.

"Complicated. Like your shopping money not really being your money. But you tried to stop them. Why? You have a death wish, taking on people like that?"

"I'm not a criminal. I mean, I didn't mean to be. I just got caught up with the wrong crowd. I thought they were the right ones. I don't know." I glared at the pile of synthetic blond hair on the ground, angry at my own excuses. "I just wanted to be a hero."

"A dead hero by the sounds of it." Dean pushed himself to his feet and walked away, cradling his arm.

I almost took out my phone but didn't know who to call or where to go next. I sat on the concrete and tugged at the weeds, tearing them out in showers of dirt, taking my pain out on them. Jake had tried to shoot me, kill me. He'd definitely kill Dean if he saw him again. Everything told me if I wasn't with Jake, I was against him. He'd come after me. I couldn't go home; Jake knew where I lived. I'd given him the address. He'd been there, seen my parents, manipulated them.

I had no money left for travel or accommodation and didn't know the area well enough to get myself moving in any direction. Tears built up along my bottom eyelashes and the first broke free, splashing on the ground and turning the concrete the color of Dean's eyes.

"Do you have somewhere to go?" he asked.

I looked up, and Dean stood next to me again. I shook my head and another tear spilt.

"Come on then."

14

Dean and I both moved slowly. I jumped at every sound, expecting a gunshot or an empath to burst out from behind a corner and attack us.

Dean kept a steady pace but wobbled as he walked. He'd lost a fair bit of blood and must have felt woozy. I'd be woozy just from the pain with a hole in my arm like that. I offered my shoulder for support, and the second time I did, he accepted.

We only walked two blocks, to where a trailer park spread from the end of a cul-de-sac. Dean pulled out his keys and let us into a mid-sized trailer, permanently fixed in place like most others around it. The screen door rattled and inside, a man lay sprawled across the couch.

I stiffened and looked to Dean. He just shook his head, put a finger to his lips, and led me past a kitchenette piled in beer cans and a tiny bathroom to a room at the end. The man let out a gurgling snore as Dean closed the door behind us.

His room barely passed eight-by-eight feet in size, with a small bed, beanbag, and set of drawers taking up most of the space.

Dean scooped up an old towel from the floor and held it against his bleeding arm.

Boys. I frowned and snatched it off him. "Do you have any kind of first-aid kit? Bandages or something? Alcohol? At least something *sanitary*? If you won't go to a doctor, we better clean that up properly ourselves."

Dean left the room. He returned with a box of Band-Aids, scissors, a clean cotton dishcloth and a bottle of vodka with just a finger or two left in the bottom.

He handed them to me and shrugged, then sat on the side of the bed, looking extremely pale.

"Okay, we can work with this. Can you take your jacket and shirt off?"

Dean looked away, almost as though he was shy.

"I just mean, I might need to cut them off around your arm

if you can't."

"No, I think I can manage." He let out a slow hiss of air as he unzipped his hoodie and peeled it away from the wound. I helped him pull the sleeves free of his wrists, since he worked one-handed to undress. He inched his T-shirt off. It took him a while so I cut the dishcloth lengthways down the middle, and started working around in a zigzag line to turn one half into a long strip. I dropped the makeshift bandage on the bed and soaked the other half of the cloth in vodka.

Clenching my teeth against nausea, I bent forward to inspect Dean's arm. A mixture of running, dried and coagulated blood created a gory horror-show. I dabbed around the mess on his bicep until I could see the bullet hole clearly. I leaned so close to Dean I felt his body heat radiating off him and his breath against my face, contrasting with the cool chill he gave me inside. The smell of blood mixed with the smoky-musk scent I noticed on him before. He didn't smell like a smoker. Maybe just someone who lived with one.

With the blood cleared, I saw a clean hole passing straight through the edge of his muscle. *Thank all things sweet and fluffy I don't have to pull a bullet out.* Just half an inch to the side, and the bullet would have missed him completely. A couple of inches the other way and I didn't want to think about it.

I'd just finished cleaning it off when it started bleeding again.

Dean spoke, his voice low. "You okay? You're turning all kinds of green."

I nodded but didn't open my mouth to reply, worried I might throw up.

I stood back up, away from the blood, and took a deep breath. I held up the bloody wash cloth. "You have another clean one?"

Dean started to get up but I put my hand on his shoulder. He took the hint and told me where to look in the kitchen. I walked back into the room and cut a second cloth in half as well to make some padding for the entry and exit wounds. Then I started wrapping his arm.

I felt Dean's eyes on me. I tried to focus on the bandaging.

"How about your cheek?" His breath tickled the fine hairs on my neck.

"What about my cheek?"

Dean lifted his uninjured arm to the left side of my face, but didn't touch me. I placed a hand there myself and felt a sting. The first shot Jake had fired. I remembered a pain on my cheek at the time, but then I saw the dead woman and people started screaming, and Jake kept pointing his gun and the world was upside down... I'd completely forgotten about it. My hands shook as I looped the bandage around Dean's arm.

"Is it bad? How's it look?"

"A thin line, just a graze I guess. Doesn't look like it bled much. You were lucky."

Maybe my empath powers had helped it heal fast. Maybe it would have been healed completely if it weren't for Dean's blocking. I wished I understood it all more.

I sighed and tried to wipe blood from my hands with the already soiled cloth. "Yeah, well, we both must be lucky since we're not dead. You should have just run. You wouldn't have been shot at all. Why didn't you run?"

Another shrug. No emotion I could read in his face or body language.

My first-aid results looked pretty dismal when I was done. I stuck the bandage closed with half a dozen adhesive band-aids. At least it didn't seem to be bleeding through yet.

Dean stood up and pulled a clean T-shirt from the drawers near the bed. He faced the other way as he put his shirt on in slow, careful movements. Muscles on his back shifted under the skin and I couldn't help but notice how nice his body was. With the baggy clothes he wore, I'd had no idea. I blushed, a mixture of embarrassment for looking and anger at my thoughts. How I'd stared so lustfully at the empaths' attractive bodies.

Them and their workout routines, creating those pretty shells.

"You work out?" I asked, sounding cattier than I meant to.

Dean finally had the shirt over his shoulders and let it drop loosely to cover his chest. He turned back toward me. "I *work*. I do some cash-in-hand jobs for a construction company. Manual labor stuff. Keeps me fit."

He reached into the drawer again and seemed to dig down through to the back to extract a packed of painkillers. He popped a couple out and swallowed them without water.

My thoughts became ragged. I was so angry at myself it overflowed onto Dean. I had no one to blame for my part in that messed up situation but myself, but if Dean hadn't been at the bank, maybe guns would never have come out. It would have been in and out. Easy pickings, like Emma had said. No one would have gotten shot.

No one would have died.

"Why were you even at the bank? Were you following me?" I snapped.

Even without being able to read his emotions, I could tell from Dean's frown just how dumb I'd been. The bank wasn't far from the mall and park, but we drove and went around in circles for ages while I got my wig right and panic buckled down. Dean could have walked to the bank in that time, but it was unlikely he'd followed us in Donny's jeep.

"The world doesn't revolve around you," he said. "I don't know where you're from, but this is my town; that was my bank. I was in to cash my dad's welfare check. I try and do it myself if I can so it doesn't all go on... my dad."

The shake in my hands had spread up my back, up my throat, and my head shook. "I'm sorry, I—"

"Who were those guys? What was the trigger-happy fashion model talking about, about blockers and powers? Why was he set on shooting me? And don't tell me it's complicated."

"They're empaths, like superheroes, but they weren't super-heroes. I just thought they were superheroes and that I was like them and I went with them but they weren't. They were the bad guys, and you're something else as well that does stuff to our superpowers..." I kept babbling. I shook and tears streamed down my face, stinging the graze on my cheek.

Dean put his hands on my shoulders and I rattled under his touch. "Okay, you're really freaking out."

He steered me to the unmade bed and sat me down. I scooted across to sit with my back against the wall and pulled the covers up around my shoulders, trying to fight the chill racing through me.

"You're in shock. Maybe something hot will help. I'll go

see what we've got. Put the TV on and just try and relax a bit."

I squinted at the small, blocky television sitting on the cluttered top of the drawers. "Where's the remote?"

"Doesn't have one."

"Really? Retro much? You can't even give this kind of box away anymore. I know. My mom has tried." I tried to smile a bit and lighten the mood, but my teeth chattered and I must have looked a little insane. I imagined how my hair must look after its release from under the wig and the mental image rounded out nicely.

"It's a whole two feet away. I'm sure you can manage."

I tried to follow his instructions and not be completely useless as the guy with the bullet wound looked after me. Dean had made me a hot chocolate by the time I worked out how to get the television on. I set the volume extra low, worried I'd wake his dad.

Dean went to take a shower, to shake off his own shock and clean up some more blood. I told him to keep his bandages dry if he could, but didn't know if that would help.

I settled into the blankets with the mug of hot goodness balanced on my knees, and my shaking became less intense. I still felt teary, confused, and sick to my stomach. The news report on the TV didn't help.

The bank robbery was the top story.

They showed some security-camera footage, but it was too distant and grainy to make out any details. I had been right, though. The old woman Jake shot was dead.

Was that my fault? If I hadn't stepped in front of Jake and he hadn't swung the gun away... no, then Dean would be dead. If Dean wasn't there, they might never have brought out the guns. But if I hadn't drawn attention to him, they might not have spotted him in the crowd. If I'd refused to go at all, the whole thing might not have escalated. Or Dean would have been dead. I was like a hamster on a wheel, going round and round. *I could go crazy thinking like this.*

I thought the news report was over, but it continued. Footage from another scene I recognized, the warehouse fire. Warehouse fire and theft, apparently. While one building burned, valuable goods had been taken from others nearby. There was evidence of arson. The news reporter said police felt confident linking this event with the bank robbery and other crimes in the area over the last month. The pattern also matched crimes from a number of cities previously. They used the term 'terrorist cell' and I pulled the blankets up closer around my face.

I hadn't even questioned Donny and Jamie loading the car at the fire, or the extra luggage when we flew back from my earthquake-stricken hometown.

They were looters, but worse, even setting up disasters to take advantage of the emotions, making bad stuff happen on purpose. Not once had I seen them do anything heroic. I'd just assumed they did and they'd let me believe.

Even Jake. Would he have even saved me if I wasn't one of *them?* He said he saw some of the fight before he helped. How long did he wait and watch until he decided to step in, to make sure I was one of them, just because he wanted another 'path on his team? What if I'd just been a regular girl in trouble?

I heard the shower still running through the thin wall between Dean's room and the bathroom. Dean was shot. *I* was shot. Someone had *died.* It was a nightmare and it didn't even faze Jake.

Just what else had he done in the past? What was he capable of?

I had to stop them. The only way Dean and any other victims of these villains could be safe was to shut the team down. Permanently. Block off their powers for good.

Jake said Dean could do that.

How? I had no idea. Dean probably didn't know either. He didn't seem to know what was going on at all. He might not even want to help.

I finished the hot chocolate and put the mug on the drawers next to the TV. My eyelids felt leaden and sound of the running water calmed me.

But maybe Dean could learn how to shut down empaths. He could practice on me. I would give up my powers.

I'd give up the whole superhero fantasy if it meant everyone was safe again.

15

stared at the screen of my phone. I'd been staring at it since I woke up. Half an hour, according to the clock. I'd tapped in my home number but couldn't hit Call.

Dean slept across from me on the beanbag. I'd fallen asleep in his bed before he got out of the shower and the idiot hadn't kicked me out like he should have.

He curled on one side, holding the bandage on his arm with the other hand. It didn't look comfortable. I noticed no coldness from him while he slept, but couldn't read any emotion from him either. That could have just been because he was asleep. What did I know? It wasn't like I'd had training with this stuff.

I sighed and looked at my phone again. I should call my parents, but at this point what could I say? *Sorry for leaving, I'll be back as soon as I take down a bunch of superpowered criminals.* Yeah, that wouldn't freak them out at all.

The beans in the beanbag rustled and hissed like a snake. Dean shifted and opened his eyes. I gave him a shy smile in return. He probably felt more awkward with me here in his bed than I felt. If he felt anything at all. His expression was blank. The coldness crept into me again.

I turned the phone off to save battery and put it down on top of the drawers.

"Morning. You calling someone?" he asked.

"I was going to call my parents." I took a deep breath. Time to sell Dean on my plan. "But I want to finish all of this first."

As calmly and as rationally as I could, I started from the top, trying again to explain the empath powers, who Jake and the team were, and what Jake had said about Dean being a blocker.

Dean looked skeptical.

"I know you think I was babbling like a crazy thing last night, but it's real, the powers, the whole thing. I need you to believe me."

Dean seemed to think for a moment. "Then show me."

"I *can't*. You're a blocker, remember? When you're around,

you stop my powers from working."

"I'm not doing anything on purpose."

"I know. But that's how it is. At least, unless you're surprised by something, or unconscious."

"Well this is all pretty surprising stuff, but you still don't have superpowers."

I folded my arms. "I don't know exactly how this stuff all works, okay?"

"Okay. Let's work it out then. What sort of range does my... *blocking* have?"

"Oh! Right, maybe I can demonstrate the superpowers from a distance. Good idea. Let's go outside and I'll see what happens. I'll still need some strong emotion to tap, though. Anger or fear emotions are easiest."

"Sure, okay." He still looked unconvinced, but I was grateful he was at least humoring me. "But you probably shouldn't go out looking like that."

Dean dropped his gaze to my chest and I blushed. Then I looked down too and saw the crusty bloodstains across the front of my trench coat and shirt that I'd slept in.

Dean dug out what he assured me was his smallest T-shirt and I went into the bathroom to change and clean up.

I peeled off the old clothes, and after giving myself a quick wash down, tried to clean them off too. The blood rinsed easily off the plasticky material of my trench coat, which I was happy about since it was almost the only thing I had of my own now. The white peasant blouse was unsalvageable.

I put on the shirt Dean had given me. The fabric was old and worn to super softness and there was a picture of a cartoon super-critter on the front. *Is he having a laugh at me?* I tried to tuck the shirt in, tie it to the side, do anything to make it not look like I wore a tent. Nothing worked, so I just left it untucked.

Dean paused and looked me over before we left the trailer. "Looks good on you."

He said it in the same matter-of-fact tone he'd used when he complimented my smile the day before. I just shook my head and tried to cool my face. I never understood why guys liked girls wearing their shirts. Wearing a guy's T-shirt felt like the most unflattering fashion ever.

It wasn't too early, but no one else seemed to be out and about in the trailer park. Still, it turned out finding some anger to tap proved easy. Just a few trailers down the sounds of a domestic came clearly though thin walls. I stood outside, and Dean backed away until I felt the cold leave me. I gave him a thumbs up.

I let the heat of emotion radiate into me, trying my best to absorb it efficiently, and my muscles burned with strength. A stop sign across the laneway seemed like a decent target for a superpower demonstration.

I checked Dean was still watching, grabbed the pole with both hands and put my foot against the middle. I pulled with my hands and pushed with my foot, and the solid metal pole bent easily in half.

It felt good to be so effective with my powers, and I couldn't resist a smile when I saw Dean's jaw drop. I had probably looked the same when Jake had demonstrated his powers by smashing that bench. *Ugh. Way to break a mood.*

I didn't even care then how much work someone must have put into the careful mosaic artwork on the bench Jake had destroyed. Neither had Jake. He'd just demolished it to make a point without a second thought. *I should have realized then what I was getting into. Destruction of property isn't exactly good-guy behavior.* But I'd been blinded by surface things, not to mention dazzled by an empath much better at this stuff than I was.

I felt bad for having busted an important street sign. I strained to straighten the pole, which proved harder than bending it in the first place. Once bent, it just wanted to remain crooked.

A red flash caught the corner of my eye. I turned to look

down the long laneway through the trailer park toward the road that passed the other end. Jake's Maserati cruised by at a speed designed for scoping.

In a blur, I dashed back to Dean as fast as I could until my powers waned in his presence. I still had just enough momentum left when I reached him to push him out of the middle of the lane and into the cover of the nearest trailer.

"Okay, I believe you!" Dean said, looking down at where I had my hands still on his chest from pushing him. I dropped them away and gave him some space.

"No, it's them. The car down there."

"The ones from the bank?"

I nodded. "I don't think they saw us. But that was them, looking for us. It's why I need your help."

"My help?"

"Yeah. I have a plan."

We waited until the Maserati had continued on, then we snuck back to the sanctuary of Dean's room.

The minor effort of our excursion had left Dean looking paler than normal. Some blood showed through his bandage, and I worried it wasn't healing right. He took the last couple of painkillers from his drawer.

He took a seat on his bed and I paced in the small space

in front of him while I presented my plan. A plan to block Jake and his team's powers for good.

As I thought, Dean had no idea how to even begin blocking an empath's powers permanently.

"That's why I want you to practice on me." I looked into his gray eyes, and spoke as earnestly as possible. "You can learn how to do it by locking away my powers."

He didn't respond. He just stared with his usual blank expression.

"Look, I know it's a lot to ask, making you learn how to do this and take on those guys, but you saw how dead set Jake was to get rid of you. It's the only thing I can think of to keep you and others safe, so you can protect yourself properly. Without, you know, turning to assassination or something. We can't even call the cops on them—not while they still have their powers."

Dean nodded. "I understand. I can try, but it still feels kind of crazy. I don't even know where to start."

"Me neither," I admitted. "I only really found out about my own powers last week. I know less about yours. It's not like there's an Empaths Help hotline. We just have to experiment, I guess." I slumped down onto the beanbag. "When I use my powers, it feels like sun warming my skin, filling me with energy, spreading heat through me. When you're around, I just feel cold."

Dean made a face. Normally, I would know exactly what that meant, but without my powers, as far as I knew, the emotion could be anything from anger to just passed gas.

"I just mean, if energy is warm, it's like a cold lack of energy. Can you, I don't know, try and visualize projecting more coldness?"

It felt stupid even as the words came out of my mouth, but Dean tried anyway. I could see him concentrating, but nothing seemed to change.

We gave up and had toast for lunch.

Dean's dad wasn't around so we sat in the living room. It smelled of stale beer and weed. I pretended not to notice.

"Why are we even like this?" Dean said with his mouth full. "I mean, how do we even have these powers? If I understand them more we might get further."

I tried to piece together the few bits of information I had. None of it sounded particularly scientific in hindsight. "Well, for empaths, we just sort of absorb excess emotion from people and it makes us stronger."

"So you're like emotional vampires, feeding on other people's life force."

"That's silly."

"Fine, leeches then, or some kind of parasite."

"Harsh."

"Okay maybe, but really, excess emotion? You think people don't need every bit of the emotions they are feeling? That anything you can tap into is just fair game? That it's yours to take?"

"I..." I hadn't thought of it like that. "I just thought the powers were part of being a hero."

Dean had inhaled his toast and pushed crumbs around the empty plate with his finger. "Pretty people, hot cars, wads of spending money... was that your idea of being a hero, too?"

"Just the perks?" I fake smiled, toothy and pleading and not even caring about my crooked teeth. I was being lectured, but I deserved it. Dean had a way of seeing things I'd been blind to. I needed to hear what he thought. "What is your idea of a hero?"

"Someone who doesn't think about themselves, who puts others first always, even before their own life. Someone like..."

Dean stood up without warning and dumped his empty plate into the sink. He paused there for a moment then came back to sit next to me on the couch. I chewed my toast slowly and stared at the floor, wishing I could understand Dean more. Without my emotion-sensing powers, all I had were questions.

Really hard-to-ask questions.

"I wish I knew how you were feeling." I blushed and rambled on. "I just mean, something has made you block all your feelings away, so much it extends out and blocks empath powers too. There must be a reason. If I knew more about how, or why, it might help."

Dean made eye contact for a moment before returning his focus to the stained carpet. I didn't want to push too hard, so I took a different tack.

"Maybe if you could work out how to let emotions out a little, it might be easier to also pull them in more, create a more powerful block than your normal one. Something that could lock down an empath permanently, like Jake said blockers can do. Do you think you could try letting some emotion through?"

Dean shook his head. "I don't think I can just... do that."

My suggestions weren't working, and Dean seemed less and less interested in trying them. And very uncomfortable talking about emotions at all. But he had let emotions through in the past, or at least had been surprised out of holding them back so much they blocked my powers. In the alley, and when he was shot, he was too shocked to keep a tight rein on his feelings. I hadn't actually read his emotions those times, but I hadn't exactly tried. Other things on my mind and all. If I could just surprise him again now, I could see what happened, see what he was really feeling.

But how could I surprise him? I didn't know why I thought the first idea that popped into my head seemed like a good one, but I acted on the impulse before common sense or embarrassment could stop me.

I leaned over and pressed my lips against Dean's.

They were soft and cool and spread slightly under mine. My eyes fluttered closed and a shiver crept over my scalp. Then I felt the coldness leave me and I opened my eyes, surprised my impulsive action worked.

Dean's gray eyes looked into mine, inches away, just as surprised.

I focused on reading any emotion I could in them, drawing them into me. What I felt was heavy with depression, a sadness as deep and hard as a glacier. Hiding within it was something small, tentative and warm. Something guarded so closely I couldn't identify it. I moved my lips back away from Dean's. His breath was fast and hot on my face.

The sadness I'd tapped overwhelmed me, like a heavy weight around my chest dragging me into black water. I backed away to the other end of the couch, shaking my head like I'd just been boxed in the ears. "Too much... bad feelings..."

I could tell Dean felt confused, hurt, and then the icy chill spread through me again and I couldn't read him anymore.

He finally found his words. "You did that just to get my guard down?"

"And it worked, yay?" Clearly not yay. "I'm sorry; it was just an idea that came to me. Your emotions were just a bit much for me to handle. But I'm sorry, anyway. I shouldn't have done that, or I should have asked first. But I couldn't have asked first or then it wouldn't have surprised you."

"It's okay. It doesn't matter." Dean had closed off completely. He didn't look sad, or upset. He didn't even look angry. He had gone back to complete emotional shutdown. But now I knew on the inside he kept hidden a deep well of grief, pushed down, out of sight. Emotions I couldn't even handle for a few moments. No wonder he blocked them away.

I could tell his life wasn't easy. Everything around us screamed poverty. His dad didn't seem to work, and was possibly an alcoholic.

Dean came across as smart, and able, and so... kind. Even when he'd pressed me on acting spoiled, which he'd been right about, he could easily have been much crueler. With the pain he held inside, I was surprised he wasn't.

I tried to smooth things over with Dean. He didn't talk

much for the rest of the day, but remained cooperative, nodding and trying a few more suggestions to practice his powers. We tried some visualizing techniques but honestly, they just felt wanky. It was still early when Dean started looking gray and tired, and I could tell his bullet wound troubled him.

We ended the day frustrated and without any headway on locking down my powers.

I insisted Dean kept his own bed and I curled up on the beanbag. He fell asleep before me, and for a while, before I found my own rest, I stared at him, remembering the sensation of the deep, black despair he kept hidden inside.

16

Thursday morning, I woke up to Dean trying to tiptoe around me.

"What time is it?" I asked, squinting at the window. The mostly bent blinds didn't block much out but barely any light showed through them.

"Six thirty. I need to get to work." Dean put on a dark-blue hoody with holes at the elbows. "I'll be back about three."

"What? No." I bolted upright in the beanbag. It shifted under me and I almost fell on my side. "You can't. If you're out working all day, Jake might find you."

Dean sighed and didn't look at me. "I have to work, Livvy.

I didn't even get to cash Dad's welfare check this week, and I'm out of money."

"No, I won't take any arguments. You can't work anyway, not with your arm like that. I bet it's hurting." I said the words, but my stomach cramped with guilt. *Out of money?* Not only had I been taking up all his time, eating his food, and getting him in trouble in the first place, it was also my fault he couldn't get to work or a bank. I had just come from Jake's mansion where the staff handled everything and cash was handed to you in rolls. Even before that, at home with my parents, I'd never had to worry about running out of money. I had an allowance and my parents bought me whatever I needed. I knew, sort of, that some people lived day-by-day, only just earning enough to get them by, or sometimes not enough. But this was the first time I'd ever *felt* how privileged I had been. Part of me wished I hadn't handed the change from my shopping trip back to Jake. That would have made things a bit easier right now—although it was stolen money. *Why did everything have to be so complicated?*

I'd work something out. I had to stop being the spoiled brat and start working harder for Dean.

Dean sat down on the bed again with a slight wince.

"Yeah, I thought as much. Can I have a look at how it's healing?"

Dean nodded, and took his hoodie back off.

I lifted the sleeve of his T-shirt. The shoddy bandaging was twisted and had a bled through. "We should put a clean dressing on it. Or at least that's what people seem to do in movies. Then you can walk me into town and I'll see about some cash."

"And that will be safer than me going to work?"

"I'm not going to rob a bank, if that's what you're thinking. If you show up at a construction site with a bullet hole through your arm, people are going to talk and Jake will find out who you are and where to find you. I don't plan for us to be out long, and at least if I'm with you, I could knock you out or something and use my powers to get us out of there if things go wrong."

"Well, you have worked out one way to shock me out of my blocking ability," Dean mumbled.

I blushed and went to get more makeshift first-aid supplies. There weren't many left, and they felt so inadequate. Once I got some cash in town, I'd purchase some real bandages and dressings. I made a mental note to also buy him some more washcloths to replace all the ones we'd used up.

I unwrapped and gently cleaned Dean's arm. It didn't seem to have gotten any better. The skin around the wound looked red and yellow and inflamed. I bandaged the area with the last clean washcloth available in the trailer, and Dean walked me into town.

It proved hard trying to walk casually while still keeping an eye out in all directions for Jake and the rest of his team. I felt like an exaggerated cartoon character, sneaking up to corners and ducking when cars came past. But no one seemed to pay us any attention, and we made it to the main street without any sign of the other empaths.

The bank was closed up, police tape webbed across the front and flapping in the slight breeze. My stomach seemed to flap the same way. Dean had lent me one of his hoodies since it was cold but I couldn't wear my too-obvious red trench coat. I hugged the worn, soft fabric to myself and smelt him on it.

I went into the pawn shop I saw last time I was here and sold my white-gold heart pendant necklace. I got less than half what my parents had originally paid for it, but it was something. Enough to get by a couple more days. I only hoped this would all be over by then.

I asked Dean about somewhere good to eat, and he took me around the corner to a tucked away diner with a drug store conveniently next door. I bought a first-aid kit which had bandages, dressings, and everything we should need, then went into the diner, insisting on buying lunch for us both.

The diner had a mix of cracking plastic table sets and a line of tall booths along the wall. It was still early for lunch so the place was practically empty, and we took a booth in the far back corner that looked nice and secluded.

I bullied Dean into ordering something substantial, sure his body needed it, and after I set aside what I needed to pay for lunch, I slid the remainder of the cash across the table.

"What's that?" He was already shaking his head.

"It's for you."

"I can't take that."

"Sure you can. It's your pay. I'm paying you to work for me, to keep trying to do this blocking thing. If you can't get to your job because of me, then I'm your job."

We locked gazes, both unwilling to budge, the money sitting untouched on the table between us.

The waitress arrived and put a massive hamburger down in front of Dean, and two milkshakes that came in tall retro glasses in the middle of the table. My fish and fries were in an actual basket, the paper lining it spotted with grease. The waitress raised an eyebrow at our strange stand-off.

I smiled at her, then pouted. "I'm trying to pay him back and he won't take it."

She wiped her hands on her apron and flicked her curly

hair. "Just take the cash, kid, before I consider it a tip."

Dean pocketed the money begrudgingly and the waitress left us to our food.

"As long as you don't make me call you Boss," Dean muttered.

"You're no fun," I teased back, but couldn't crack his façade.

Dean took a big bite from his burger and chewed it for a while. "You didn't have to sell your pendant. Didn't it mean something to you?"

"Other things mean more."

I picked through the fries and battered fish bits. They were good, but I didn't have a big appetite.

Dean seemed to barely be putting up with my presence. I wasn't surprised, considering the trouble I'd brought him, not to mention crashing his space and sleeping in his room. Each day, he seemed more and more irritated sharing close quarters with me. Or maybe it was my crazy plan and nagging to get this to work. But we had to succeed. At every moment I worried Jake would find Dean, or go to my parents to find me.

He had to be stopped before he hurt anyone else.

Back in the trailer after lunch, Dean and I sat in the living room and tried again to practice his blocking abilities. We attempted turning them off and on, making them stronger or weaker, but nothing worked.

Dean's wound bled through a second time so I rewrapped it with the new proper dressings and the result looked a lot more professional. I hoped that meant it would also heal better. I didn't like the way it was looking one bit.

Dean was just putting his shirt back on when his dad stumbled in the front door.

"Just finishing up with your little whore?" His words sounded slurred.

I winced. I had no idea how to deal with an angry drunk. I liked him better when he was passed out and snoring.

"Dad, don't." Dean stood up as a buffer between the two of us.

His dad's gray hair was greasy and while his eyes were the same shade as Dean's, they bulged, bloodshot, and gave him the look of a crazy man. They fixed on me over Dean's shoulder.

"I know you been sniffing around last few days. I see it's going on. Don't think you can go shacking up here. No money to be sniffing for anyway, and you can't be having more of my drink."

I opened my mouth to try and defend myself but just shook my head. I looked to Dean for a cue on what I should do, worried how embarrassed he might be. I got nothing. I might as well have been a figment of his dad's drunken imagination.

Dean put a hand on his dad's shoulder, leading him like a

sleepwalker to the room at the opposite end of the trailer to Dean's. "Why don't you go lie down for a while?"

His dad swatted the gesture away. "You two stole my vodka! Don't try and hide it. I know what's what and what's gone. You get rid of that whore, Dean. Get her out before she goes leaves anyway! Just like your mom."

He turned the other way and left out the front door again, cursing and stumbling.

I sat speechless on the couch.

"Sorry." Dean stared at the closed front door and didn't look like he would turn around anytime soon.

"Is that it? Is that why your dad's like that? Because your mom left?" I blurted. I clenched my shaking fists. Dean hadn't stood up for me. He'd just let his dad call me a whore and rant like that to my face.

Dean remained still. "She didn't leave. She died."

"Oh, crap. No, I mean, I'm—" Sorry didn't cut it. I was such an idiot. I should have realized, from the amount of pain Dean carried inside him, that it was something more. All that pain, and I was angry at being yelled at.

"I'm so sorry." I said the words anyway, even though they weren't enough.

"He wasn't always like that. He just couldn't handle the

way she left." Dean leaned on the back of the door and still didn't face me. My heart warmed and ached for how he was defending his dad. I had no way of understanding what they'd been through. I'd never lost someone close. I wanted to poke, to pry, to encourage him to keep talking, but decided keeping my mouth shut was the best option right now, in case another foot tried to squeeze in.

The silence extended and I thought he might not have anything else to say. He stayed leaning on the door. I stayed watching anxiously from the couch.

Finally, he spoke.

"My mom got sick. Like, never-getting-better sick. We weren't badly off and Dad gave everything, every saving, every dollar he'd earned on any kind of treatment he could find. Everything, and more. Dad refused to let her go, refused to give in or stop doing whatever it took." He spoke softly, slowly, as though he were calming himself before each word. "The medical costs bankrupted us. We lost our house just to keep Mom in hospital in palliative care."

He shook his head, as though he could deny the past. "She didn't want to be there. She faded, slowly, painfully, and steadily. She was ready to go and knew what the drawn-out illness was doing to our family."

Dean didn't move. His words held just the smallest edge of pain.

I mopped up flooding tears with the neckline of Dean's T-shirt I was wearing. I kept quiet, didn't sob, but the tears just ran.

The sadness I'd felt in Dean when I kissed him all came back to me. How long had his mother's illness gone on? What had their family been like before? What had Dean been like before? I'd never seen him really smile. I bet he was gorgeous if he really smiled. It would reach those gray eyes and they would sparkle in a way they never did now. The neck of my shirt was sodden.

Dean's next words came a long moment after the others.

His voice broke so slightly I wondered if it was my own imagination.

"Mom took her own life."

I'm sorry. They were such useless words, so flimsy. What everyone says when they don't know what to say.

I thought back to my parents and the strength of their love. If what happened to Dean's family happened to ours, under those circumstances, would they break? If I lost one of them, and then lost the other to alcohol, I doubted I'd manage half as well as Dean. I'd up and left them behind for this adventure gone wrong, but only because they were so permanent. Like no matter what I did, I could always go back to home, to comfort, and there they would be. Even when distant, my parents were a safe place in my heart. The idea of losing them seared my insides.

If that happened to me, I would probably lock all my emotions away too. Stop myself ever having to risk loving and losing anyone again. Do anything to hide from that pain.

Dean shifted and I wiped frantically at my face to dry it in case he turned around.

I stuttered, hoping my words weren't completely useless. "I'm sure that she didn't want to leave you behind. If she thought she had any other choice, I can't imagine—"

"I know. I know she left so her illness, and Dad's obsession with saving her, wouldn't destroy us completely."

Our conversation from the day before came back to me.

"What is your idea of a hero?"

"Someone who doesn't think about themselves, who puts others first always, even before their own life. Someone like…"

When he clammed up, was he going to say someone like his mother?

I couldn't emotionally grasp what it must have been like for her, to feel like the burden of her illness did more damage than her choice to leave. It must have been an impossible decision. It seemed like Dean's dad wasn't going to accept her death either way. And despite Dean saying he understood, it had clearly broken him as well.

And yet he was still so strong. Opening up to me, telling me all of this, couldn't have been easy. My voice broke as I said, "Thank you, for sharing that with me."

He faced me and I shivered.

I grew colder inside than his presence had ever made me. Anything Dean had opened up, he'd now closed again tighter than ever before.

He sat back next to me on the lounge and asked about what we were going to try next.

I casually caught another tear with the flick of a finger and suggested we take a break and spend the rest of the day watching TV.

We sat close, our shoulders just touching enough to share warmth between us, but inside, the sensation of cold only grew.

That night, I wriggled myself into a semi-comfortable position on the beanbag again before Dean could say anything about sleeping arrangements. He came back in from his shower and stood still in the middle of the room for a moment before getting into his bed.

"I'm sorry," he said. "For being angry that night we first

met. For not saying thank you for what you did."

I didn't know what to say. I had obsessed over it at the time, but when everything went crazy, I'd forgotten about it again until he brought it up. It just didn't seem to mean so much anymore. "That was you angry? I was the one yelling like a lunatic."

"I was angry, and I'm sorry."

"It's okay, really."

Dean paused, his jaw clenching briefly. "It's just, I saw this mousy girl—"

"Hey!"

"—willing to take on two big guys, willing to risk her life to save a stranger. To do something like that, you have to be someone special. It made me so angry, the thought that someone so special could have been hurt, for someone like me."

"I guess I was just trying to be a hero." I shrugged, trying to make it seem like nothing. I hadn't done it for him, not really. I'd done it for myself, to be praised. I'd had no idea what it meant to be a hero, not then.

"My mom taught me what a hero is. And she taught me that heroes die."

My gaze drifted down to the bandages on Dean's arm. How he pushed me clear of Jake's gun, how he preferred to be beaten to a pulp by those bullies than have me risk myself to help—he seemed determined to save me from what he thought was a hero's fate. And at the same time, he was taking that path for himself.

No. I wouldn't let him. My breathing grew fast and my eyes burned hot, and tears fell before I could hide them. "Your mom did what she could with nothing to work with but tragedy. We've got superpowers. I'm going to make sure we both survive this."

Dean reached across and wiped my tears from my cheeks, then turned away.

Neither of us said anything else.

The next morning, I woke and saw Dean sitting on the side of his bed, watching me. His expression was intense, yet calm. Longing, yet withdrawn. Something inside felt different, a turmoil of hot and cold, and then it happened.

Ice grew in me, crystallizing and encasing every sensation of empath power I knew. And then I felt nothing at all. Not the warmth of absorbing emotions, not the cold of Dean's blocking. *Nothing.*

I ran through the trailer park, trying to connect to any emotion outside of my own but nothing came.

It was done. Dean had learned how to shut down an empath permanently.

I was normal.

17

At night, the overgrown park across from the mall felt like a scene from a horror movie. The wooden play fortress loomed in the shadows and a slight breeze made tree branches creak against each other. Streetlights at either end of the space provided lighting, and both flickered. It was cold and my red trench coat swirled in the wind like a cape. I pulled it closed over the T-shirt I wore—*Dean's* T-shirt. It smelled of him and my heart beat a little faster.

This plan had better work.

I kept imagining every possible way things could go wrong. The idea of Dean getting hurt following my plan made anxiety dance like a jittery sickness inside me.

I hoped the cold would give us an advantage, so Jake and his posse wouldn't sense Dean's presence until too late.

I'd called Jake earlier that day. He wasn't happy to hear from me, and I'd begged, I'd begged shamelessly to be given another chance to be part of their team again. He hadn't been as interested in me as he had in finding the blocker. He'd sounded obsessed.

"Where is he? You know, don't you?" he'd snarled over the phone.

"I don't know where he is. We went separate ways after the bank. I'm sure you don't have to worry about him anyway."

"Every blocker is worth worrying about. Every one needs to be put down. We are *better*, better than any normal human, and those blocker scum drag us down to nothing. They are the enemy."

"I know, and I should have listened to you before. Please, give me another chance."

"So you think you can manage it now, doing what we do? You want it bad enough? You got us into all kinds of trouble with your stunt at the bank."

"I'm sorry." The words tasted disgusting in my mouth. I was glad he couldn't sense my emotions over the phone. "I screwed up big time."

"Why would we even want you back on the team? What do you have to offer? Maybe if you could tell us where the blocker was, we'd consider it. But if you really don't know—"

"Fine, okay, fine." I'd let him think he'd called my bluff, but this was just the bait I needed. "I helped him get home, so I know where he lives. I'll tell you where you can find him. But only in person."

Jake had been more than eager to arrange the meet-up then.

I shivered, and wondered what time it was, whether the team was late. I felt like I'd been here for hours. But Dean and I did get to the park much earlier than we needed, to give Dean a chance to get hidden.

The kid-sized hiding spot looked uncomfortable, particularly with his arm still hurting him so much. He'd suggested the park while I'd tried to think of somewhere with a place Dean could hide, public but without other people around. Somewhere that wouldn't seem more suspicious to the team than I thought this already must.

A car pulled up beside the park. Not one of the team's usual favorites, but it was them. My blond prince charming who had turned from beauty to beast strolled up followed by his pack. They seemed confident and I sighed in relief. It meant we'd cleared the first part of the plan that could have gone wrong. They could have sensed Dean the moment they got here, but either the cold night was masking his presence, or Dean was able to hold in his blocking power.

He said he thought he could do that now. He seemed sure of it. I'd only realized that Jake's team sensing his effect could be a problem after Dean had already locked me down, so we had no way to test what he could do. But Dean said he'd worked something out. He had something inside now he could use to control his abilities. Now I just had to hope he could keep holding in his general block and still individually shut each of the team down for good.

Jake wore a dark leather jacket over a stark white designer shirt. He stared at me with disdain. I marveled at the face I'd once thought so dreamy that now spoke of nightmares. His attraction-based hypnosis powers had no chance on me anymore. Unfortunately, his general intimidation levels still worked.

"So, uh, hi. Um." *Wow, lame start.* I had to get my brain working, keep them engaged, talking, so Dean had time to do his part. But Jake and the team were so daunting, they flicked the off switch in my head.

"Oh honey, living rough?" Emma almost sounded sympathetic as she smirked at me and my slept-in clothes. She, of course, looked ready to hit a red-carpet afterparty—minidress, stilettos, perfect blow-out and all.

"Yeah, things have sucked on my own." That was a direction I could take, playing to their egos. "I should never have left you guys."

Donny was frowning. "Jake—?"

Jake waved him silent, his eyes remaining on me. "I'm surprised you didn't try and go home," Jake said coldly, and my heart whumped. Had he checked? Had he done anything to my parents?

I tempered my emotions, trying to stay calm. I had to keep them here, keep them talking as long as possible. "Who could go back to normal life after this?" I gestured to them, as though they summed up everything normal life couldn't give me.

Jake nodded like I'd spoken gospel. "So you understand we have to find and stop the blocker?"

"Totally. Who would ever want to lose these powers?" I had to turn the conversation back away from finding the blocker again, because the moment they pressed me for his location, they'd know something was up.

Donny looked more and more uncomfortable as we spoke. He tried to get Jake's attention again but Jake kept shushing him, too busy enjoying a good gloat at my expense. *Come on, Dean.*

I scrambled for more words. "At the bank, I didn't know what I really wanted, and it messed everything up. I thought I was doing 'the right thing'." I emphasized those words as sarcastically as I could. Jamie scoffed at the very idea. "But who says what's right anyway? If we're stronger, better, if we can easily take the things we need—why not? Isn't that evolution? We deserve to be happy."

"Wow, sounds like she finally gets it." Emma laughed.

"Yeah, but she doesn't deserve it. Not until she tells us where to find the blocker." Jake strode around me in a circle, a panther waiting to snap. He must have been able to tell how uncomfortable this whole situation made me. I hoped he thought it was just nerves in his oh-so-glorious presence, the bastard.

"Yeah, of course. I'll tell you. But how do I know you won't leave—"

"No buts. Tell me!" Jake came to a stop behind my back. He groaned softly. "What is that? I feel..."

Donny looked off-color, drained. "I've been trying to tell you, something's happening. I think the blocker is *here*."

Jake grabbed me and turned me to face him, shaking me. "Is he here? Did you bring him here?"

Last-ditch effort. I shrugged, but my shoulders shook with fear. "It's probably just the cold you're feeling."

Donny stared at his hands, his expression distraught. "I think he's locked me down. I've lost it all."

Jake shoved me away in disgust and yelled at the others. "Find him! He's got to be close by."

Jamie moved in a flash. Dean mustn't have gotten to him yet. He sprinted around the park, checking the perimeter, behind trees and fences, in high grass. My teeth bared in disgust knowing it was my fear he was using, stealing from me, to get that speed.

Donny moved slower. He went to the play equipment and wooden fort. I tensed, and tried not to watch and make it obvious where Dean hid. As he climbed through it, Donny's adult footsteps clunked heavily on the timber. I hoped for a plank to snap under his weight but no such luck. Still, they weren't finding Dean.

Emma watched Donny's slow, normal movements for a moment with her mouth agape. Her voice held pure terror. "I can't. I can't lose my powers. I can't go back."

"Snap out of it, Ems. Help us find the damned blocker!" Jake hissed.

She looked at him only briefly. She met my eyes for a second too and I saw a strange moment of hesitation. Without my empath powers, I didn't know what it meant. Then she fled.

She moved so fast she was just a blur till she reached their car and took off in it on her own. So much for team loyalty.

Jake growled and pulled a gun from the behind his back. He pointed it at me, and his hand shook. "I'm not losing this power, Livvy. You're dying first."

I'd known Jake wouldn't be shy about turning to guns once powers failed them. The bank job had taught me that much. Dean had figured as much too, and didn't like my plan with him hiding and me in the firing line. So I'd come up with a back-up plan that comforted Dean's concerns for me, but I wasn't so sold on it actually working. I just had to do anything I could to keep Dean safe until Jake and his crew were all locked down.

I threw the back-up plan out there and hoped it would fly. "If you shoot me, you're done. I've given that phone you gave me to someone, and if I don't show up safe by midnight, they have instructions to turn it in to the cops, along with all your numbers, that lovely happy snap of us, and notes on all of you and your activities."

Jake's face became a feral mix of snarl and smile. "You think I care about that? I've still got plenty of cash to get away clear and can change my face if I have to. But I won't have to. I will still have my powers, and with my powers *I* am the law. You hear that out there, blocker?" Jake called into the park where Donny and Jamie still hadn't found Dean. He kept the gun held in front of my face. "The second you shut me down, this girl is dead. Crawl out of wherever you're hiding and we can all just sort this out."

I flicked a glance at the wooden fortress, at the join between two sections of the construction that had been badly patched up when the original builder's plans didn't line up quite right. The planks shifted.

"Dean, don't!"

The wall hinged open, revealing a standing-room-only space, and Dean stepped out and walked toward us, holding his hands up in a gesture of surrender.

Jake whipped his gun away from me and fired.

No hesitation. No time to stop him. No time to talk him out of it. No time for anything.

He shot Dean, just like that.

18

The blast of the gun echoed like thunder around me. I ran to Dean, but it felt like a dream where everything was too slow.

A look of shock hung on Dean's face and he stopped still. He stared at his chest like he couldn't believe the way the blood pooled and spread across the fabric of his shirt. Like he'd spilled ketchup on himself, and might just laugh with embarrassment and brush it off.

Then his legs buckled.

I ran. I was too slow.

I skidded under Dean just before his head hit the ground,

catching it in my lap. But I had been too slow to have stopped the bullet, to have pushed him out of the way, to have saved him.

Dean's skin was more blue than pale. He kept his teeth clenched, panting between them.

"Help!" I screamed into the night uselessly. If the gunshot hadn't brought anyone, my scream wouldn't either.

His chest bled so much.

I tried to hold it in, pressing down. The blood oozed out between my fingers.

I let out a wheezing cry.

"Liv?" Dean grasped for one of my hands. "Listen. I'm sorry."

"Sorry?" Nothing made sense. He'd done nothing wrong. His apologizing lips were spotted with blood. *This can't be happening.*

"Sorry. For pushing you away. Being scared of you. Of feeling for you."

Jake yelled at me, a muffled hum, unimportant. Only Dean mattered. But Jake kept yelling. "Stand back up, Livvy. I want you facing me."

I didn't want to hear him. I only wanted to hear Dean, to keep hearing him talk so I knew he was still okay.

"Didn't want to feel like that. To risk losing someone again.

The feeling—" He coughed, winced. "Too intense. Shutting that down, that gave me control of these powers."

He held me trapped in the gaze of his gray eyes. "But I don't want to anymore, don't want to shut it away. Not if… I'm dying. I want you to know…"

"You're not going to die. Heroes don't have to die," I sobbed.

My chest burned. The fierceness of what I felt for Dean, the pain and pure need, blazed through me. And not just my feelings. Emotions came from Dean as well, intense and raw, warming me throughout like a nearby fire.

"Livvy, I—" Dean breathed.

Arms, hard like steel, yanked me away from Dean and I screamed like I'd been torn apart. Jamie pinned me up against him, pulling me back. I kicked and wrenched my body around but his grip was charged by emotion. Emotion he stole from me. My pain. *How dare he?*

"Let me go! Let me go back! Dean!"

Jamie dragged me toward Jake. I struggled against him, useless—at first. But he felt weaker and weaker.

No. I was stronger.

Any ice inside me that had shut my powers away had melted. Power unfurled within me, wild and mighty. That warmth of emotion, shared between Dean and I, that *feeling* … he'd used it to unlock my powers again.

Along with my powers came hope. Now I could fight back, get help for Dean, save him. There was still time. *Please, please let there be enough time.*

I tore one arm free of Jamie's grip and turned so I could see Dean again.

I had to let him know it had worked. That everything was going to be okay.

His eyes were closed. His body gave a startling shudder then went still.

I let out a sound between a scream and a roar.

That *feeling*. That warmth. It was love.

I'd fallen in love with him. Had he been trying to tell me he felt the same?

I screamed again. I ripped into Jamie. I clawed his arms off me. Donny came to help him, unpowered, but still strong and twice my size. I sparred back, ducking their blows and kicking, scratching, jabbing between them with more strength than they could ever know. I drew the power from myself, from the fury of my own emotions, not stealing the scraps from others.

Jake kept his gun aimed our way, but didn't seem to want to take the risk of hitting one of his own. I was surprised he had even that much moral fiber. He stashed the gun and came to join in by hand.

I knocked back Donny just in time to be grabbed by Jake. I pulled free from him just in time to take a hit to the ribs from Jamie. I held my ground between the three of them, outmatched but determined.

I fought for my life and for Dean's, if it was still there. Dean had taught me what it meant to be a hero, a real hero. He'd taught me kindness, and selflessness. He'd been right; heroes weren't the fake fairytale dream I'd thought they were. But he had to be wrong about heroes dying.

I couldn't accept that.

I loved him. I couldn't lose him.

I chanced a look at him again, hoping, wishing to see him pick himself up, to be okay.

Dean still didn't move. He looked dead.

Jake caught me with a blow to my jaw that slid me back along the ground. I didn't even feel it. I launched myself at the men again, feral with grief. I didn't hold back, unleashing all the overwhelming emotion surging through me. I broke ribs, snapped knees, pulled arms from their sockets.

I set loose all of that emotionally charged energy against them but still the pain inside me grew.

I knew despair like I never had, like I couldn't begin to handle. A black, bottomless pool drew me in like quicksand, drowning me.

Darkness overwhelmed me. The despair fed on everything I had inside, consuming any feelings of morality or mercy.

And it remained ravenous.

I turned it on Jake, Jamie and Donny, and I let it feed. I used that black energy to tear into their very beings, absorbing everything I could from them. All their power, all their energy—I stole every emotion from their bodies.

They fell to the ground like human husks. Just pretty shells.

My mind reeled, burned, darkened, then lit up like an exploding fireworks factory. My muscles were a flash fire of pain. My only thoughts were for Dean.

I stumbled a few steps towards his body.

Then I fell too.

19

Everything was too bright. Too loud. Machines beeped and whirred. Colors bled through my closed eyelids.

Why was there so much pain?

I remembered the night in the park. I remembered Dean being shot. I didn't remember what had happened next.

I stirred, and when I opened my eyes I found myself in a hospital bed, strung up with tubes attached to the back of my hand and wires stuck to my chest.

I was alone in the room except for a petite, dark-skinned nurse who leaned over me to press the call button.

She smiled at me as I blinked myself awake. Golden energy

glowed off her. My head pounded and I winced.

"There you are. Came back to us. Shh-ssh, don't move. You've been out for a while. We'll get a doctor in to look you over."

Her smile hit me like a solid wall of energy, the sheer strength of her happiness making me nauseous. Who was ever *that* cheery? All around me, emotions seeped through the walls from people celebrating, people grieving, people fighting enemies in their own bodies to stay alive. Every emotion invaded me, crawled into me like tiny spiders digging under my skin.

I rolled over to the side of the bed.

The nurse must have seen me turn green because she was ready with a pan to catch my vomit.

She had helped me clean up and was taking my blood pressure when a doctor came in, bringing a billow of orange, blue, and purple emotions with him.

Am I going crazy?

I leaned back in the bed and took deep breaths, trying to slow the spinning inside. The doctor started checking me and my attached machines.

"Good to see you're awake. You have some nausea?"

I nodded only slightly but my head hummed with pain. "What happened? Is Dean...?"

The doctor took a seat next to my bed and pulled out a notepad. "We were hoping you could tell us what happened. No one else has been able to after how you were all found, with one boy shot and you and three others injured and unconscious."

I looked down at my hands, remembering the fight, the blows I'd taken. There wasn't a mark on me.

I remembered the blood spreading across Dean's chest.

One boy shot. "Is he...?" I couldn't say the word aloud.

"The cops are flustered too. They've identified the shooter from the bank robbery, and the two other men carrying guns are his associates. But they are very curious to know how you and the boy who was shot come into it." The doctor glanced across to the door, where out in the hallway, a uniformed officer was pacing, looking back to the doctor for his cue to come in. "But you don't have to talk to them yet if you don't want to."

My mind raced over all the evidence of my involvement with Jake's team. Photos, phone calls, texts, leaving home, my stuff at their place, the video from the bank. I had to tell the truth, as much as would be believed. That I didn't realize who Jake and his companions were until it was too late. It was going to be a long story, and a long investigation, and I couldn't handle it now. I could barely think.

"Can't now. Later." I turned my head away.

The doctor nodded and gave the side of my bed a sympathetic pat. "Of course. Whenever you're ready." He paused, tapping his pen on his notebook. "But, if you can give me some idea of what happened, I'd appreciate it. Anything to help understand what is causing the symptoms in the others. They aren't unconscious anymore, not really. But they are completely catatonic, all three of them. We can't get any response. Their brain activity is almost completely non-existent."

Just pretty shells.

I could tell him what happened, now I realized what I'd done. *I killed them.*

Or I might as well have. I ripped all their emotions right from their bodies, leaving them as vegetables.

I bent over the side of the bed a second time, my eyes watering and my chest convulsing. The nurse held a pan out for me again and I retched, but nothing came up. My body rolled inside with pain and guilt and I wished I could vomit it all out, clear all these feelings from me.

I had taken lives.

And at the same time, I had somehow absorbed, stolen their powers. That was why everything was amplified. Why I felt everything so much more vividly.

I deserved this torment, the screaming of every emotion around me drilling into my skull. It could send me insane, and I almost hoped it did.

I only had to know one thing first.

My voice was a harsh scratch, and I spoke to the floor, still bent over the side of the bed. "Did he die? Is Dean dead?"

My heart grew small and painfully tight, waiting for the answer.

The nurse replied, "He's been in and out of consciousness since surgery. He almost—"

I was already moving, throwing back the sheets, tearing drips and wires off me.

The nurse tried to talk me down. The doctor stepped in front of me to urge me back to bed. I shoved him weakly, and he flew back against a wall, bringing a beeping machine down with him. I was much stronger than I realized.

"Sorry!" I clenched my teeth as my body ran riot with overloaded emotional power.

I bolted out and down the corridors, not giving a thought to the state of my hospital robe. I followed my nose, or rather, my heart.

I felt him, felt his presence, before I saw him.

I stumbled into the room Dean lay in, grabbed his hand,

and dropped my head onto his shoulder.

I found quiet there.

Next to Dean, the pains and pleasures of others were muffled. I wept with relief.

"Hey." Dean's voice was dry and husky.

"You're alive. You're awake," I whispered into his shoulder.

"Yeah, you too."

I didn't feel any coldness—just soothing warmth. He wasn't holding back. He wasn't keeping any of his emotions from me, but he still calmed me with the abilities he'd learned.

The love I sensed from him made me weep more, but happily. I wished he could experience how I felt for him in return.

I lifted my head from his shoulder and kissed his lips.

The kiss was gentle, lingering, and I put everything into it that I couldn't give justice to in words. It tasted of salt tears and summer days, heating us both with glowing joy and desire.

He put a hand around my waist and pulled me onto the bed next to him. He let out a small grunt of pain when I pressed against him but still kissed me harder.

I pulled my lips away just far enough to talk. "I'm sorry. You okay?"

"Worth it." He smiled like I'd never seen before, and his gray eyes sparkled as they stared into mine.

I heard shuffling from the doorway but couldn't turn my eyes away from Dean's.

"Livvy?" It was my mom.

Her voice, and the jolt of worry it contained was enough to pull me back from Dean to see her and Dad.

"Mom!" Tears filled my eyes. They came in and hugged me. I tried not to break them when I squeezed them back.

My nurse cleared her throat and stepped into the room as well.

"We just arrived but you weren't in your bed." Dad frowned, and nodded to the nurse. "Tara said you'd just run off, and probably come here."

Tara looked from me to Dean to my parents, crossed her arms, and said, "Five minutes, then he needs to rest again."

She took a quick glance at Dean's heart monitor then left us in peace, tapping her watch on the way out.

I still clung to Dean's hand, but my parents only had eyes for me, looking deep into my face as though they'd find written there what they needed to understand everything that had happened. A soft cyan halo surrounded them.

"We came as quick as we could." Dad smoothed my hair back with his hand. He explained how they'd been so worried when I'd disappeared, but then my 'friend' had shown up and

161

explained I was fine and I'd be away with him for a while.

"It seemed to make sense at first, but the longer you were gone, we couldn't understand why we'd accepted some stranger's explanation." My mom's voice was choked, as though she were the one apologizing to me, as though they had failed me. "When we found out you'd been brought into hospital—"

"It's not your fault." There was so much I had to explain, to fix. I wanted to tell them everything, but I had no idea how. I tried to keep it simple. "I made mistakes and fell in with the wrong crowd. I'm sorry. But I'm still here. I'm okay."

My mom nodded, then looked past me, down at Dean, and our tightly joined hands.

"And this boy, was he part of the wrong crowd?" Her tone wasn't accusing. It was soft, tentative with care.

"No. He's the one who saved me. And I saved him."

20

I hadn't slept very well since the whole final confrontation-with-evil-super-powered-villains thing happened.

I had to keep using those words. *Evil. Villains.* I had to use them to stop myself feeling awful for what I'd done to them. It didn't really work.

I'd spent almost every minute by Dean's side since we were admitted to hospital. Our little romance and bizarre brush with death was the gossip of the staff and came with a mix of sweet sympathy, coos of cuteness, and tuts of "just a silly teenage thing."

They didn't understand that I really might die without

Dean by my side. After whatever I did to Jake, Donny, and Jamie, everything I sensed, every emotion of the people around me, hammered into my brain like the drummer of a death-metal band thrashing his skins.

There had been other changes as well. Everything was strange and different and painful. It was only near Dean that I found solace. The hospital staff didn't know; they just saw my puppy-dog eyes for him and, as long as I didn't interrupt his care, let me camp out in the armchair in his room.

My parents were great about it all. I knew there would be a big talk with them down the road, but for now, they were just being here for me, and letting me be here with Dean. Mom and Dad took shifts so at least one of them was with us during daylight hours, but often they had to duck away to get back to the contractors repairing the house and Mom's shop after the quake. We were still in Dean's hometown, and since we didn't own a car they'd had to hire one, and had been driving two hours each way to be with me.

I felt guilty as all get-out about it. But it made me love them even more.

On top of that, I wasn't sure what was happening with health insurance, or what the extended stay in hospital and all the tests were costing, or whether Dad's leave from work was paid or unpaid, but they were being good adults and organizing everything so I was oblivious to the details.

I even had a visit from Terry, my parents' cop friend. I was sure he was more curious about the case than my wellbeing because he asked a bunch of questions about Jake's team and what had happened in the park. Apparently, he'd recently been promoted, so maybe he was practicing his detective skills. Maybe he thought he was helping my parents out with answers. I don't know, but it was beyond awkward so I was glad when he left.

The doctors didn't know what was wrong with me, which made them hesitant to discharge me. To them, five kids came in bloodied and unconscious and only two had woken up, and I'd woken up as a gibbering mess. I tried to act as normal as possible and not let on anything to do with the whole super-powers thing, but it was hard with my mind so messy. Not sleeping wasn't helping the issue.

I'd like to say I was getting used to the lumpy vinyl armchair in the corner of Dean's hospital room, but it was just as much of a torture device as it had been three days ago. Still, I slept—or tried to—in there beside him rather than go back to my room down in a different ward.

I needed to be by his side.

I *wanted* to be by his side.

Daylight streamed in through the blinds despite them being drawn, but I was exhausted from another night of broken sleep and stubbornly kept trying to snooze. Dean's cocktail of heavy-duty medication meant he slept easily and often, his body working hard to mend the damage from Jake's bullet.

"Mumble, mumble, tests, mumble, mumble." A voice reached my sleeping mind.

"Huh?" I tried to swallow, my mouth dry and tasting like hospital. My eyes didn't want to open. Maybe I'd dreamed it. I tried to let sleep take me again.

"Wake, mumble, mumble, time, mumble, mumble."

I groaned, exhausted.

I thought it was a nurse. I remembered something mentioned yesterday about tests. Right. I had to have some scans done. The doctors were still trying to work out what had happened to me and the others, what with the weird comas and all. *Sure*, I tried to say, but just flopped my head forward in a vague nod and tried to stand up.

"Poor girl, mumble, happened, mumble, recover, mumble."

A soft squeaking sound approached me. I was barely conscious, yawning and trying to get my stuck eyelids to open as Tara, the petite nurse who'd been looking after me, put an arm around my shoulder and helped me into a wheelchair. The one that had been sitting nearby for Dean's use since he was under strict no-walking orders.

I wanted to argue I didn't need the wheelchair, and something else, there was something else I needed to argue. But I was already being wheeled down the hall.

I couldn't turn my brain on. There was too much noise in my head. I tried to wave back at the nurse but she kept pushing me along. I shook my head, trying to clear it, but the pressure was building too quickly.

"You okay, love?" Tara slowed down to check on me, but it was too late. I wasn't sure how far we'd walked, but I knew it was too far.

I was awake now. And I was too far from Dean. Too far from his blocking powers, and my head felt like it was going to explode.

Because of this place, this hospital, full of people who were sick and dying, and the loved ones of people who were sick and dying. People who were angry at the world for their prognoses. Women in the pain of labor and experiencing the elation of meeting their babies for the first time. People about to go into surgery, or even simply preparing to receive an injection. And without Dean to block my powers, every one

167

of those scared, sad, angry, or elated emotions came flooding into me at four times the strength it should have.

I wasn't just an empath anymore; I was four empaths.

And it was too much.

Not only did the power from the emotions rampage through me, but now I could *see* them. Flowing streams of shimmering and juddering colors. Auras that haloed bodies and reached out to me like iron filings to a magnet when I passed by.

Wincing in pain, I reached back and clutched at Tara's hand. "Go back." I pleaded the words out, and they were followed by a rough cry.

My vision blurred and my head lolled back. The nurse crouched beside me, flashing a light in my eyes. She spoke, but I couldn't hear past the pounding sound in my ears. With a concerned look, she started pushing the wheelchair again. Faster. In the wrong direction. *No. No, wrong way.*

The world spun around me and my veins and muscles felt like they were about to burst. I grabbed onto the arms of the wheelchair and felt the plastic split and crumble, the metal bending like butter in my fingers.

In the swirling faces around me, I saw a familiar one. *Dad.* The expression on his face said everything about how I must have looked. He ran down the corridor towards me.

"Take me to… Dean!" I tried to hold eye contact with him but kept wincing from the waves of emotion. I needed him to understand. I used every last bit of my focus to get the words out. "Must. Be. With. Dean."

Dad turned away from me, looking to the nurse for answers as she continued to push me along. She didn't have the answers. *Dad, listen to me!*

I pushed myself out of the chair as it was still moving. The force of my action knocked Tara and the wheelchair across the corridor. The momentum was too much for me too, and I landed facedown on the ground. I could feel myself losing control of my body, my muscles jerking and seizing from the uncontainable influx of energy.

Dad knelt on the floor with me, cradling my head as my body shook and I slipped into unconsciousness.

I didn't know how long I was out for, but I slowly came to. The first thing I saw was Dean, his body bent with pain, supporting himself on his IV stand. He was so far away, but I saw him like a beacon, the lighthouse to the storm of emotion raging through me.

I blinked, the rest of the world coming into focus. There were nurses all around, checking on me, on him, and on Tara where I'd sent her flying.

"So sorry," I whispered to her through clenched teeth. She looked embarrassed more than anything, as though she'd somehow caused this with a self-destructing wheelchair. Everyone seemed at a loss to explain what had happened. I guessed 'that girl's got superpowers' was pretty low down on what most people would believe.

Dad looked down at me, frowning, but he sighed with relief when I looked back. He glanced across at Dean, then back to me, then to Dean again. Dean was pushing through the chaos to get closer to me. His nurse was following behind, scolding him for being out of bed, but he didn't listen.

He knelt on the ground next to me, those blue-gray eyes calm yet intense. "I woke up and you weren't there. Came to find you. Figured I should just follow the signs of chaos."

"Thanks," I replied. "I hope you didn't bust your stitches."

"I'll survive. Looks like you needed, well..." His sentence faded out.

Him. I needed him.

I smiled my thanks. I swallowed my guilt at being so dependent on him.

Dad was halfway through a discussion with the nurse about my seizure.

"This is exactly why we need to do the tests," she said.

"She needs to recover first," Dad argued.

"I'm fine. I'll be okay, really. I can do the tests. But …" I looked to Dad, hoping he'd understand, "… can you and Dean both stay with me?"

21

Dad could have said no to letting Dean tag along to my tests. But he didn't.

I wasn't sure how much he saw, or believed, or understood from when I collapsed, but I saw him talking to Mom when she came in, and I saw them talking to the nurses, and I saw forms being signed and arrangements being made, and suddenly I was moved to a private room right beside Dean's. Well, my belongings and medical charts were moved. I'd remained right by Dean's side. I didn't want to suffer through an experience like that again. And I liked being near him. He made my heart do a soft, gentle *flutter-flutter*.

Having my own room, my own bed, with only a thin wall between myself and Dean made a huge difference. I got to sleep and wow, I'd really needed that.

It was hard at first. My mind still wouldn't turn off and I found myself reliving the moment Jake shot Dean and what happened after, and my half-asleep self would turn the moment into a nightmarish vision of vampire me sucking the souls out of the people who'd wronged me.

But soon I did sleep, and it was long, and deep, and much-needed.

The next day I shuffled around into Dean's room. I felt sheepish, knowing he could have his privacy now. And maybe he wanted it after having me by his side every moment recently. But he greeted me with a small smile. The kind of small smile that from him, I knew, was huge.

Dean was poking at a tray of hospital food.

"I never used to understand why people complained about hospital food. When I was a kid, I loved sharing my mom's food when I visited her."

I moved closer and sat on the bed beside him. I wanted to be even closer, I wanted to hold him through what must have been a sad memory, but it was always hard to tell with Dean. He'd changed a lot, and was so much more open. But he was still Dean.

"Now I'm a bit older... yeah, I can see what people mean about this food being awful."

"You're still eating it anyway," I pointed out.

He looked at me with his mouth full of fruit jelly. "Well, yeah."

My heart swelled happily at his display of typical teenage boyishness. He seemed to be healing well.

"Want some?" He pushed the tray closer to me.

I'd just had my own breakfast but grabbed a piece of chewy cold toast to nibble on anyway.

"Okay, so," I said, trying to get focused, "I've got Detective Phillips coming in this afternoon. And I have no idea what to tell him. And I don't think he'll be satisfied with the *I'm not ready to talk yet* response again."

Dean put his plastic cup of fruit jelly down. "How much are you planning to tell him?"

"I don't know. I mean, I want to tell the truth. I don't want to lie. But that's only going to make me seem crazy. I can't really prove it, and what I can prove about my powers, well, I'm not sure I *should* be proving that. Feels like revealing that could come with way too many consequences, you know?"

Dean nodded.

"But the police are still wanting some kind of answer though, for how we all ended up out there, passed out in the park like that, and why the others still haven't woken up."

"What else could cause something like that? Drug overdose?"

"Been screened for that already. It's one of the tests they ran straight away."

"Gas leak?"

"Out in the open? And how do the broken bones get explained?" I cringed, having flashbacks of our fight. I never thought I could be so violent.

This would be the third time the police had come to talk to me. The first I'd just said "later," and considering the state I was in, they'd accepted that. The second time I'd tried to explain that all I did with Jake was hang out, and I hadn't known they were criminals. Or at least not until it was too late. I'd already embellished the story beyond the truth. I'd blushed when I lied and said Jake was obsessed with me, which was why he'd come after us and why he'd shot Dean.

After he'd shot Dean... that was when my story fell apart. And those were the answers the authorities were still waiting on from me, that I knew the detective would be pushing for the next time I met him.

"Hypnosis," I suggested with a sly shrug. "I'll tell them Jake was a master hypnotist or mentalist type, and he'd manipulated us all into a death cult and made us attempt to commit suicide by not breathing until we fell into self-induced comas."

"Wow." Dean raised his eyebrows, impressed. "Yep, that's the winner."

I half whimpered, half sighed. "I am so screwed."

22

Detective Phillips sat across from me in my new hospital room, adding a strange elegance to the place with his neat suit and well-groomed appearance. I was tucked into bed, messy hair on display, giving my best impression of 'poor girl still recovering.' Dad stood beside me. Or 'loomed protectively' would be more accurate.

Dean had offered to be here as well, but I didn't want any added stress for him. I'd bet anything he was probably sleeping right now, and I knew he needed it. He'd done his time with the detective already. All the police really wanted from him was a finger pointing at who pulled the trigger.

They seemed to want a bit more from me.

I looked Detective Phillips in the eye and knew I could manipulate him, make him think and do what I wanted the way Jake had done to me. The detective may not have been physically attracted to me, but power rushed through me and emotions blazed from him that I could use to smooth through all his defenses. But I didn't want to. I couldn't manipulate someone like that. Not unless I really had to.

"The moment this goes beyond what my daughter is comfortable with, I'm calling in legal counsel," Dad said to the detective.

"Of course, Mr. Mirawi." Detective Phillips flashed a 'just think of me as a friend here to chat' smile. "Now, Olivia, has anything more come back to you from the night in Stanford Park?"

"No. Sorry." It was the best option we could come up with, after going over ideas. Saying I simply couldn't remember anything seemed safest.

I waited anxiously for the questions to continue.

Detective Phillips just nodded. "I've been talking to your doctors, and while they don't know what caused your collapse, they say it's likely that brain function would have been impaired at the time, so amnesia is completely understandable. I won't press the issue, but if anything does come back to you, it's important to share any detail, even if it seems small."

I tried not to look too relieved, but then I realized he wasn't leaving. He had a tablet device in one hand and swiped to scroll through whatever he was looking at. "We've been reviewing evidence surrounding the bank robbery and the surveillance video corroborates your testimony that you weren't aware of what was going to happen. It's a little blurry at times, but we could still clearly see you trying to protect the people in the bank."

I gulped, knowing it had all been caught on video. The reminder of that awful event sent my stomach plummeting. "It was so horrible. I couldn't believe they were like that, that they would do those things. After the bank, I didn't want to see them again, and we only met them at the park because I was trying to talk them into turning themselves in, to stop what they were doing." It was a small lie, but still a lie. I blushed and I wondered if the detective had worked out my tell yet. "I guess that wasn't the right decision, but I didn't know what else to do."

Dad put his hand on my shoulder. "You could have come to me and your mom, Lollipop. You know you can tell us anything. We could have helped you."

I nodded, but knew I couldn't have gone to them. Not that time. They didn't understand the danger it would have put them in. They didn't know the whole truth.

"I have another video here to show you, if you think you're up to it," Detective Phillips said. His expression was calculated and my shoulders tensed.

Another video? Of what? It was clear I was only going to find out by agreeing to watch it here with my Dad. But then what would he discover about me or empaths?

I was still gaping, unsure, when Detective Phillips turned his device around, the video already running on the screen.

It showed a hospital room with three bodies laid out on life support. Two gorgeous and blonde, the third statuesque and dark-skinned. Jake, Jamie, and Donny. I frowned, looking from the screen to the detective, confused as to what I was looking at, when movement on the screen caught my eye and there was Emma, standing over the beds. She watched them for a short time, then the image changed to the view of a corridor at night. The video quality was good enough that I could see the room number. Dean's room number. And Emma stood there, staring through the small window in the door. The expression on her face was not a nice one.

"She was watching us? When was this?" I gasped.

"Can you confirm that this is the same girl from the bank? That she was part of this group?" the detective said.

"Yeah, that's Emma. Sorry, I don't know her last name."

"That's all right. We already have her details—just wanted to confirm it with you."

"Has she been caught?" Dad asked.

"No, we're still looking for—"

"Is she a risk to my daughter? Shouldn't there be an officer on protection here?"

The detective didn't seem guilty at all as he said, "There's been a plain clothes officer outside the whole time."

To protect us or to keep watch? I wondered, worried about what they might have seen or heard, and why they had kept their presence secret.

"We're doing what we can to apprehend the other girl," the detective continued. He put his tablet away and stood. "Thank you for your time, Olivia. I will be in touch, but feel free to contact me first if you do remember anything that could help us bring Emma in and help keep you safe."

23

The hospital courtyard was small and enclosed on all four sides with glass and brick, and filled mostly with people sitting and drinking coffee. But the grass was soft, and the trees created a soft, dappled-green light around us that lifted my spirits.

Dean sat on a bench about twenty feet away from me. He was off his drip and had been told to get some gentle exercise, so we walked slowly down from our rooms to get some fresh air, and do some testing. I needed to see how far his influence on me extended.

I took another step backwards and winced.

"There it is." I wandered back to Dean and sat next to him. "That's about it. I mean, I might be able to push a bit farther, but that's the point when things start hurting."

I rubbed my temples. "Hospital is probably one of the worst places to have enhanced emotion-based powers. *So many* intense feelings here. Maybe out in general public I could get farther away before things became too much for me. And at some point, I'm guessing I'm going to have to go back to high school."

"Do you think it will be as bad as in hospital?"

I gave Dean a look that showed what I thought about the emotional levels of people in a high school. I made a little whooshing sound and mimed my head blowing up. "I need to get this under control though. I need to be able to be away from you. Not that I don't like being with you—I mean, I do—but I'm sure you don't want to be forced to follow me around all the time, and really, we only just met each other, and now we're like, squish, together, with the close-proximity thing all the time and..." And I was rambling.

"I really don't mind," he told me softly. "Really."

My heart fluttered and I fidgeted with my fingers. "It's not ideal though. I don't want you having to feel responsible for my sanity like that. It's too much."

Dean nodded, his expression vacant.

"Maybe you could block me again. Permanently. Then I wouldn't have to deal with any of this. I'd be normal."

I glanced over at Dean as he thought through my proposal. He was still so pale, and a small shine of sweat on his skin told me everything his lack of expression didn't about the pain he was still in.

"But what about Emma? What if she comes back, decides she wants revenge or something? I'm safe; I can block her if she comes after me, but if you're normal again, you won't be able to protect yourself."

"Then I'd need you to stay close by anyway. So no solution there. But to be honest, if she comes after me again, I kind of want to have my powers to fight back with."

I hung my head, kicking at the dirt under the seat. My hand rested on the bench right beside Dean's and he lifted his little finger and placed it over mine. We hadn't really touched much, or kissed, or done anything romantic since I'd first woken up. And we hadn't really talked about that night. What he wanted to tell me. What I felt for him.

Things were kind of awkward.

But that small action, that small touch between our fingers, meant everything to me. It gave me the strength to ask more from Dean than I wanted to.

"We're going to have to work something out." I looked him in the eyes. "And to do that, I think we're going to have to tell my parents. Everything."

24

Mom popped her head around the corner of my door. She had a huge smile on her face. "Guess who's getting discharged today!"

Dad walked in beside her. "Is it me? Gosh, I sure hope it's me."

"Daaaad," I groaned. I sat cross-legged on my bed, and Dean was in the armchair by the window, as we'd both been waiting anxiously for my parents to arrive.

"Well, it does feel a bit like we've all had a long hospital stay. Aren't you ready to go home?"

I paused and bit my lip. "Not really. I don't think I can come home yet."

"Do you think she's scared about re-integrating into society?" Mom asked Dad, cheekily.

Dad looked at me, offended. "It can't be that you like the food here more than you like my cooking."

"I'm serious, guys. I... kind of can't leave until Dean leaves."

I didn't need empath powers to understand the looks they were giving me.

"It's not what you think. This isn't just about some teenage crush. There's more to it than that, and I know it's going to sound crazy, but just hear me out. This is truth time, okay?"

At the word truth, I had their full attention. Mom sat on the bed beside me, dead serious. "Okay, Livvy. We're listening."

"There's so much to tell you..." I took a deep breath and started at the beginning. I explained what I'd experienced the night of the quake, and leaving with Jake and his team. I explained my powers and how they worked. I explained how Jake was able to manipulate me, and them, with those same powers. I explained what had happened the night in the park, what had really happened, and what I'd really done. That I remembered it all, and the effect it was having on me now. I explained that was why I had to stay close to Dean.

My parents listened. They didn't say anything. But what could they say when presented with it all?

187

"I know this is a lot to take in, and I know you are having trouble believing any of it is real, which is why I asked you to bring something in for me."

Mom reached into her tote bag, looking dazed. "The phone directory? I had to ask around our neighbors to find one. What is it going to do?"

I half-smiled at my mom. "Hopefully, it will prove to you what I can do. It's my disposable demonstration tool."

I took the brick-sized book off my mum, and let the emotion I could feel nearby channel through me. Even with Dean in the room, I was still 'on.' With his blocker ability, he basically brought me back down to normal empath level. I had plenty enough strength for my demonstration, and without even flexing, I easily tore the phone book in half across its spine.

Mom gasped.

Dad picked up one of the halves and had a couple of unsuccessful goes himself, inspecting it for clues as to how I'd done it.

"It's not a trick. And you know I've been screened for drugs—this isn't some steroid- or meth-induced rage strength," I reminded them.

The room was silent for a while.

"Okay," said Mom.

"Okay?" I replied.

"Okay."

"Okay," added Dad.

"Okay," Mom said again for emphasis.

She looked back at Dad and at me and at Dean.

"Well, this is huge. Okay." She took a deep breath. "I don't know what to say."

"Congratulations on having superpowers?" Dad half-smiled, and I laughed out loud.

"This is really real?" Mom asked, and Dean and I both nodded. "Okay. I believe you. I do."

Dad became serious again. "Who else knows?"

"Just the girl, Emma. And the other guys that got brought into hospital, but... you know. I don't think the detective knows. I've tried not to give anything away."

"Good. That's smart, Lollipop. We're going to have to think about this some more, work out what it all means. But thank you for telling us. You really can tell us anything. Even when you develop superpowers, since that seems to be what you teenagers are doing these days."

"Oh, my girl," Mom sobbed and stepped across to wrap me up in a huge hug.

"Are you the same, with super-strength?" Dad asked Dean.

"It's a bit different for me. Not as exciting."

From within Mom's embrace, I said, "His power is what's keeping me stable now. He has sort of a dampening effect. That's why I need to stay near him now my powers are overloaded. Dad, you saw it in the corridor that day."

He puffed out a breath and rubbed the back of his head. "I did see something. I could see it was real, but I thought it was psychological trauma real, not *paranormal superpowers* real."

I reluctantly withdrew from Mom so I could get to the next big issue. "That's why I can't get discharged until Dean does. I figure it will be easy to make them keep me in longer again. I just have to have another seizure."

"On purpose?" Mom looked shocked. "We can probably just ask to hold off on discharging you. I know they are short on beds, but still."

"Trust me, I'm not looking forward to doing it. But Dean could easily be in here another week or two, and they won't let me stay that long without a reason. I mean, if they try and wheel me out of here, it's going to happen again anyway."

"Let us at least talk to the doctors first. We'll say we saw some odd behavior from you just now. That should be enough to get some more time," Dad said.

190

Mom took a chair by the bed, shaking her head slightly. "This is all so... Dean, how did your parents handle this when you told them?"

My whole body froze and I tried to somehow suck Mom's words back out of existence, but there was no way of dispelling the tension they'd just dropped into the room.

Dean didn't look phased, but he rarely did. He spoke calmly, and I gritted my teeth and tried not to cry as though every bit of emotion he was blocking ended up channeled into me instead. "My mom died a while ago, and my dad won't visit hospitals. We haven't told him anything. He's not very... reliable."

"He hasn't visited you?" Mom looked enraged. "At all?"

Dean actually looked worried. He shrugged and mouthed 'no'.

Mom stood back up and went straight to him, giving him a hug that was even longer and more smothering than the one she'd given me. I could feel Dean's shock hit me like a wall as his blocking abilities disappeared for a moment and a huge swell of emotions washed over me.

Luckily, he recovered quickly, and he even brought his arms up and returned the hug. No one could deny a mom hug.

"What happens once you are both discharged from hospital?"

Dad asked me, looking like he had already thought through what was going to happen next and wasn't sure he liked it.

I put on my 'please forgive me' face. "Can Dean live with us for a little while?"

25

It had taken another seizure to convince the doctors I needed to stay, but we'd made sure Dean was close enough that it didn't last too long. It still left me feeling like I was a sack full of vomiting cats.

I'd become the hospital's favorite lab rat, with various specialists going over my case and seeming way too excited about the completely abnormal and inexplicable brain activity my scans were showing. I wished it all wasn't on file, but I just had to hope there wasn't some neural marker that screamed 'this person has superpowers!'

The doctors decided to try a range of different medications, which I disposed of secretly instead of taking. I played it weak for a while after the seizure, then showed sudden improvement when the doctors started talking about releasing Dean.

It was another week and a half before Dean and I were both discharged at the same time.

I packed all the clothes and belongings my parents had brought in for me into the bag I'd been living out of. Dean didn't have anything with him to take. No one had brought in belongings for him—no clothes or necessities for his stay. He'd mostly been living in hospital gowns at first, and more recently, his nurse had found a couple of changes of clothes from lost-and-found and charity boxes for him. The clothes he'd come into hospital wearing had been cut off him during surgery and were so covered in blood they were disposed of with the biological waste.

In the wait between being told we were being discharged, and actually officially being discharged, I thought I would go mad with impatience. I paced anxiously, but knew it wasn't all just the waiting. There was something else. Something I didn't want to do, but felt I had to all the same.

I had to stand on tiptoe to peek through the small window in the door of the dorm-style ward they were in. I wasn't brave enough to go inside, but even from here, I could see them straight away. That Hollywood-crush-style blonde hair.

It was growing out now. I could see dark roots showing at both Jake and Jamie's scalps. Of course. Everything about them had been fake. The casts on their arms were real though.

Dean had come with me, but I didn't think he cared to see the person who'd shot him.

But I felt the need to see them again. To say sorry maybe, or goodbye, or I don't know. After what I'd taken from them, I didn't know what I could do or say to make up for it.

Even if they were able to hear me.

I almost pushed the door open to step in when I noticed other people in the room. Between Jake, Jamie, and Donny's bed, a doctor was standing with an older couple, going over paperwork. One of them turned, as though sensing I was watching, and I ducked down out of sight.

I figured they were probably more detectives, based on how they were dressed. Detective Phillips had told me there were others working on Jake's case, with the team gathering enough evidence to tie them to a number of crimes in the area and elsewhere. Regardless of what was going on, I didn't want to disturb people in an intensive care ward.

As Dean and I walked back to our room, I said a silent goodbye to the hospital that had started to feel like home. Now we really were going home, I didn't know what life would be like anymore. With Dean moving in, and dealing with our powers, and whatever our relationship was now, and my parents being involved in the lot of it—it was going to be complicated. I was going back home, but nothing could take me back to how things were before.

Everything had changed. *I* had changed.

I'd started out with such romantic, selfish notions of heroism. Now I had a new understanding of what being a hero really meant. The power, the risk, and the reality of danger and sacrifice.

Dean and I had survived our brush with heroism, but only just.

Doing whatever I could to go back to being normal was the best plan now. But I could couldn't deny the fire of pure power, the desire to be more, have more, simmering inside me, fueled by emotions.

My experiences with Jake's team, with Dean, had shown me there was injustice all around. I didn't want to be a hero just for heroism's sake anymore—but if I had the power to make a difference, didn't the world deserve that? And how did that fit into my everyday existence, going to school, dating Dean and being a daughter to two amazing parents?

I didn't know. I only knew that now I had changed, the world had changed for me too.

How could I ever be normal again?

CONTINUE READING LIVVY'S STORY IN EMOTIONALLY UNSTABLE

NEED MORE EMPATHS?

READ ON FOR
EXTRA CONTENT

EMOTIONALLY SCARRED

EMMA'S STORY

SELINA A. FENECH

I wish I could use magic to stop people staring at me, or enchant myself to be beautiful, but the magic powers I have are different. I'm not really a witch, no matter what the other kids call me. I'm not a superhero either, even if I do have special powers. Heroes aren't ugly.

The lime-green shade of my new school's corridors set my teeth on edge. Everyone watched me, and why wouldn't they? I was the new girl with a target right on her face. My sneakers squeaked as I walked and I felt so completely conspicuous. Cruel laminate flooring. My own body betrayed me as well. I was taller than most girls, which just made me easier to spot.

I wanted to love my bright red hair but I hated that it attracted attention to my face.

The other students stared openly at me and gossiped as they pretended to poke through their lockers. A tide of emotion followed their stares, the usual mix of sympathy and disgust that I was used to. That was my superpower — to sense how people were feeling, so strongly that I felt their emotions burrowing into my pores. I hated it. I hugged my new textbooks close to my chest and tried to ignore it.

Chin up, Emma. Don't let them get to you. You're beautiful on the inside. You're special and important, no matter how you look.

I tried to believe that my outer appearance didn't matter and that *real* friends would like the *real* me despite how I looked. But I was smart, smarter than most kids my age, and it made them think I was even weirder. My intelligence made me as much of a target as my face. I tried to act like everyone else, dress right, talk right, do all the right things. I had gone from being a child prodigy down to a C average. I stuffed tests on purpose, half-hearted my assignments, and worked harder on giggling mindlessly, and pretending I actually like music where dudes sing about their sexy bitches. Anything to just fit in.

It didn't work.

This year was supposed to be better. Operation: New Me.

EMOTIONALLY SCARRED

I finally convinced my parents to let me change schools. Well…
by convinced, I mean I was expelled from my last school when
I got into a fight with this girl who kept calling me names. I
had a weird adrenaline rush and broke her arm. Oops.

A little extra begging on top and my parents finally let me
have the mole, the bane of my existence, removed. The mole
that had made me the brunt of bullying my whole life. This
was no cute beauty mark, oh no, but a brown blob of ugly flesh
that covered half my chin. That's why I was called a witch at
my last school. Marked by the devil, dribbling sewage, fecal
face; I heard it all from the other kids.

My life was a living hell. If they also knew I could read
their emotions like some kind of freak…

But all that changed. I was going off to a new school, and
in between, I'd have the mole removed. Then it was meant to
be like in the books, where a group of great friends would
adopt me and the hottest guy in the school would fall for me.
I wouldn't be teased. I would be happy.

The whole plan plunged into epic fail. My plebian parents
didn't realize I needed a proper cosmetic surgeon for the work,
to actually make my face look like the mole was never there.
Sure the doctor removed the mole, but in its place he left a
jumbo pink scar like a deformed fetus.

Determined to be positive anyway, I came to this new school with a plan. I dressed up, smiled, and waited for people to ask, wow, where did you get that scar? And I would tell them crazy cool tales of my heroism, saving a baby girl from a pit bull attack, only to have a chunk of flesh bitten off my face. I'd say it was nothing, I did what I had to do to save a child. Beloved school heroine, here I come!

Except I didn't have a chance.

Someone knew someone from my previous school and gossip of my mole, and the botched removal attempt, became the new school joke. It took no time for mortifying "before and after" photos to make the rounds, and the fact that I'd lied about how I got the scar turned everyone against me. Not one student would even talk to me. Their hateful emotions seeped into me like poison, chilling my veins, making me ill.

I hadn't escaped.

I wish I could turn my powers off, to just ignore all those emotions for just a second. Or turn them back the other way and make everyone else know how I was feeling. Because right now, walking down this school corridor with my chin up pretending to smile was the hardest thing in the world.

My eyes stung. No way, if I cried in the middle of everyone, it was all over.

I turned to face the wall and got lucky. There was a notice board right there, covered in fluoro fliers for me to pretend to read while I got myself under control. There were fliers for cheerleading try-outs, chess clubs and the whole spectrum of other cliques that wouldn't take me.

Just breathe.

The corridor stank of bleach from a recent cleaning. If anyone saw my eyes damp and asked if I was OK, I'd say my eyes were sensitive to the chemicals. I always had an answer for everything. I just needed someone to ask.

I closed my eyes, and when I opened them again, Rafael, who I'd already identified as the most handsome guy *ever*, was leaning next to me. He had one elbow against the wall and his hand played with his sun-bleached hair. I don't blame him; my hands would love to do that, too.

Rafael had the looks of a 1950's movie star and he knew it. He played it up, wearing a leather jacket with turned-up collar like he was James Dean and said things like doll, daddy-o, and swell. Yeah, I've been eaves-stalking. Just a bit.

And here he was next to me, looking at me. What was going on? I scanned my surroundings for hidden cameras.

"Since you're new, I'll give you some advice." He spoke in my ear, closer than I'm used to anyone getting. I shivered.

"Advice?"

"Don't join the chess club," he said.

I let what must be a dumbfounded expression stay on my face and spoke slowly. "But... the checkered boards are so pretty, and I like the little horsies."

Rafael looked at me like I was a poor dumb girl and I worried I'd missed my shot. I raised an eyebrow dramatically, hoping he got the point.

A moment passed, then he chuckled at my joke and I let out a massive sigh. Internally. Externally, I kept my cool and gave a flirty-yet-coy grin. I was stupidly proud of myself. Maybe I could do this. I could be funny and charming and fab-u-lous. I was beautiful on the inside, and he would be the first person to see. And really, I'd kick ass in chess club, but I'd never let him know that.

"I'm Raf. That's the other important thing you need to know, new girl."

"Emma," I said. I extended a hand to shake his, leaving just one to hold up my books. They shifted, almost fell, and I rebalanced them in a way that squished my boobs up into prominence.

"Oops!" I giggled as though I hadn't done the whole thing on purpose. His smile in return was hungry, almost predatory.

I could sense the lusty excitement in him, but also something chilling, a darker emotion hidden under his grin.

"Careful, you'll need those, for, you know, learning."

"No problem. I can shake hands *and* balance books. Get me a job in the circus, I have the skills."

The bell rang. Too soon... I didn't want my time with Rafael to end. This was the nicest anyone had ever been to me and my heart raced with hope and confusion and the close proximity to hottest guy in the world.

Rafael sighed as the bell finished clanging. "Better move. I don't want to get you in trouble on your first day."

Right. I'd been here two weeks. Well, he's noticed me now at least. I had to give him a reason to remember me. Dare I?

"I don't mind getting into trouble sometimes, if it's for a good enough reason."

Raf bumped his shoulder into mine. "You're a firecracker, aren't you? Say, you want to meet up after class? Hang out?"

My lips trembled. "Sure."

"Come to Siren's Haven. You know it?"

I nodded, casually, like I went there all the time. Siren's Haven was an abandoned set of a failed pirate movie, still standing down by the river. I knew all about it because Dad was big into collecting movie props. Tacky replicas mostly, but real stuff too when he could.

"See you there at six, at the main pirate ship. It'll be a gas." Rafael winked at me then headed off down the corridor.

This was too good to be true. I hated that I doubted this, doubted that there could be anything about me he'd find attractive. I was about to split apart, torn between hope and suspicion.

Too jittery for class, I skipped out, went to the girl's bathroom, and did the Snoopy Dance.

Between when I talked to Rafael and the time for our meet up, everything changed. I almost didn't go. I almost curled into a ball of sobbing tears never to face the world again. Then I came up with my plan.

I took so long trying to decide what to wear that I risked being late. I ended up staying in what I wore to school that day: sneakers, black stockings with enough carefully manufactured runs to look every-day, short shorts, and an oversized dusty-red sweater. I'd spent long enough picking it out in the morning anyway and I didn't want to look like I was trying too hard by having an all new outfit on. All I did was change my bra. I also had other preparing to do, and the loose-fitting sweater worked well with my plan.

EMOTIONALLY SCARRED

Twilight lit the fake pirate town, turning grayed wood and dusty weeds varying shades of lilac. I squeezed through the hole in the chain link fence and when my top snagged on one of the cut wires I had a mini panic attack while getting my outfit in order again, covering up what the sweater hid.

I couldn't lose the shakes that had been with me since my conversation with Rafael. They only grew as I made my way to the half-built pirate ship, propped up on blocks down the path. Used spray-cans littered the road like a rainbow and I kicked them along to try and distract my nerves.

Siren's Haven had been abandoned a year ago when issues with actor contracts tanked production. They closed up shop and left it all standing while they tried to get back on track, but in the meantime it had become a playground. I climbed up the weathered wooden ladder onto the ship's deck. Empty beer cans lay scattered around the remains of fires. A couple of old lounges had been dragged in. All the signs of a regular party destination for parties I never got invited to.

Rafael waited for me, reclining on top of a cluster of barrels like a real swashbuckler.

"Hey, sweet cheeks." He rolled onto his side, shifted over, and patted the spot next to him.

"Hey." I strolled across the deck and paused at the barrels.

A foam mattress had been thrown on top of them. It made squishy noises when he moved. Ew.

"Come on, don't be shy." Raf patted the mattress again and its moldering stench reached me. "No pressure, I'm not going to try anything. I'm a gentleman."

I already knew how untrue that statement was. But even still, I wanted to give him the benefit of the doubt. Some dumb part of me still hoped that what I'd overheard wasn't true. For the part of me that despite everything hadn't yet turned bitter, I had to let this play out.

"Can I admit something?" My voice quavered, but that was ok, I was aiming for cute and vulnerable. But really I was super nervous about what was going to happen. "I haven't been here before. I want to have a look around. Can you show me?"

"A tour? Sure, doll, sure." He hopped down onto the deck with a smooth jump.

The wood squeaked in warning under us, fragile and not meant to have lasted this long. Rafael put an arm around my shoulder and led me to the prow. I hadn't expected him to touch me. My heart thudded. If he had put his arm around my waist the game would have been over.

From the prow of the ship you could see the whole film set. There were mermaids carved into the front wall of the pirate bar (which, like most of the buildings, only had a front wall). Tall grass sprouted everywhere, even from the façades themselves. There was a fake rock pool to our left, and the place might have been pretty if it weren't crumbling and trashed.

"Beautiful, isn't it?" Rafael breathed heavily into my ear. "But not as beautiful as you."

Where did this guy get his lines? I hated that they still made my heart race, even though I had no reason to believe him. Before I could mutter the obvious denial, he kissed me.

It was a small kiss on my temple, soft and a little cheeky. I lost my breath.

"Hey," he said, and turned me toward him. I let him move me as he wished. He smiled down at me and it was a beautiful smile. His emotions told me how excited he was. Excited, and smug.

He whispered in my ear. "Take your top off for me."

The last fine cobweb of hope I'd clung to snapped. I knew this was coming, but I clung anyway, and now I felt myself fall. I could stop this and leave now, or I could follow through with the plan I had stupidly dreamed that I wouldn't have to use. Rafael saw my pause and misread my internal conflict.

"It's OK, you're beautiful. I just want to see you."

I nodded slowly and grabbed the bottom hem of my sweater, lifting it up over my head.

I heard the cla-click sound effect of his camera app as I dropped my sweater to the ground.

The hidden camera finally revealed.

He held up his phone, admiring the photo he had taken. "Grade-school underwear, much?"

I had changed out my nice bra that afternoon for a plain black sports tank that covered as much of me as possible. I came prepared. I reached around to the back waistband of my shorts while he examined his photography.

He stood there, still pointing the phone at me, playing his cruel trick.

And I stood, pointing a gun right back.

Checkmate.

"What are you doing? Are you crazy?" He took a clumsy step back and looked around as though there'd be someone to save him.

"I knew. I knew what you had planned!"

After he first talked to me and I danced like a happy fool, thinking he actually wanted me, the fear that it couldn't be true took over. So I went to find Rafael, to follow him and find out more. I knew there had to be something going on with him, and I daydreamed that he just had some cool, dark secret that only I could know, like he had freaky powers too, or he really was from the 1950's. Instead it turned out that he was simply a jerk.

"I heard you talking to Gavin. Saying you had me eating out of your hands, and you were going to get a photo to blackmail me with to make me do whatever you wanted." I jabbed the gun at him as I talked, my voice growing louder.

"I knew about it all, and even then, I still hoped maybe you were just saying that to your guy as a cover but you really did want…"

I shook my head. I had to stop saying stupid stuff in front of him, as though I were still waiting for him to reveal he cared for me.

No. I had my plan. I knew this was coming, despite any crazy hopes I held. I came here knowing what I would do so that I'd come out of this on top either way.

"Throw your phone over," I said.

He did, and I deleted the photo of me.

Rafael trembled visibly. His expression was frozen but with my powers, his fear was tangible to me. He had his hands raised in front of him. I pulled out *my* phone and flicked on the camera. Set it to video and kept the gun aimed at him with the other hand.

"I want you to tell the world, Raf, what a jerk you are. A

horrible bully. Come on, I'm easy pickings, right? Go for the girl with the mangled face, why don't you."

His jaw moved, but he said nothing.

"Say it!"

"I... I'm a jerk, and a bully."

"You are. You take advantage of girls. Say it."

"I take advantage of girls."

The fear flowing off him made me giddy. I hadn't felt such an intense emotion before and it filled me with energy. A grin spread on my face.

"You're nothing but a small-dicked, derivative, misogynistic coward..."

He repeated me on cue.

"Who is about to *die*."

I squeezed the trigger and Rafael twisted like he could dodge a bullet. He couldn't even dodge the spray of water shooting from the gun. Working replica water pistols formed a large part of my Dad's prop collection.

Not all the wet on Rafael was from the gun. His pants were soaked. I giggled as I turned the video off on the phone and slipped it into my shorts pocket.

"Wow, a better performance than I could have hoped for. Now listen carefully, Mr. Popular. You're going to be my new bestest friend at school. You'll help show everyone how fab-u-lous I can be. Because if you don't, I will show everyone who you *really* are."

My plan complete, I turned to strut away, the proud victor.

I felt the change before I saw anything. The fear gushing from Rafael shifted to blinding fury. The heavy sound of footfalls charged at me.

He shoved me hard from behind and I landed on my face. The aged wood deck grazed my hands, turning them into splinter pincushions. I rolled onto my back, looking up at him. The anger on his face was terrifying, the strongest anger I'd ever sensed.

"No one is going to see that video, ugly bitch!"

He reached down, grabbing at the pocket of my shorts.

I wrestled against his hands, swatting him away.

"No way are you blackmailing me. You're going to suffer."

He slapped me in the face.

Something strange was happening with my powers. I felt Rafael's anger flow down onto me, bathing me, seeping into my muscles and warming them. I felt strong, the same strength I felt when I broke that girl's arm. The splinters didn't bother me. My cheek felt hot where Rafael had slapped me, but didn't sting. I felt powerful.

Rafael swung at me again and I knocked his arm away easily. He pulled back, shocked, and nursed his arm where I hit it.

I knew then I was stronger than him. My powers had always felt like a curse before, but now I realized they were something more. I was something superhuman.

I leapt onto my feet, grinning and staring Rafael down. He shied away from me.

That's where I should have left it. I should have made some witty comment, and walked away. But my hands balled into fists, wanting more fight. With this strength running through me I felt out of control. I wanted revenge for every painful word or look I'd ever suffered.

I kicked high and hard, hitting Rafael right in the centre of his chest.

He *flew* backward, like he was wired up for a movie stunt.

I was a witch after all.

Rafael hit the figurehead at the prow of the boat with a sound that made me feel sick. I instantly regretted lashing out, and went to help him up, to make sure nothing was broken. Even if he was a jerk, I hated myself for being so violent.

I took one step and a squealing groan came from the ship, followed by popping and cracking noises of wood splitting. I felt the deck shudder, and knew the ship would fall.

EMOTIONALLY SCARRED

I looked at Rafael, groaning as he tried to get back on his feet. My body screamed with energy. I felt strong, fast, and confident, like I could reach him, throw him over my shoulder, and leap to safety in time. But he was so far away, all the way at the other end of the ship, where I had kicked him to.

The ship lurched to the side as the hull split open and I ran for him. I leaped over holes that tore open in the deck. Something huge fell into my field of vision and I saw the main mast collapse down into my path, right in front of me. Unable to handle my new speed, I slammed into it and rolled to the side. My momentum spun me too fast and I fell from the side of the ship, tumbling to the ground.

Coughing dirt, all I could do was watch as the pirate ship collapsed in on top of Rafael.

I bolted away from Siren's Haven before the dust settled. I had to sneak back inside so my parents wouldn't see that I'd lost my sweater and come home half-dressed.

It wasn't my fault. It was my fault. It wasn't my fault. It was my fault. My brain was stuck in a loop of guilt and denial. There were too many variables, but I knew one thing—if I had held back, if I hadn't let my anger loose, Rafael might still be alive.

221

I deleted my video of Rafael for fear it could be used as evidence against me. I fretted about the sweater I'd left behind and hoped it would be considered just another piece of trash, not a clue to a crime. I plotted various excuses and alibis for if I was questioned. I had answers for everything.

But no one came for me.

A week later, I went to the funeral.

The grief I felt from Rafael's family ached, pounding into my skull, and I told myself it was the punishment I deserved. But not everyone grieved. Two rows in front of me, gleeful relief came from a small huddle of girls from school. I wondered what Rafael had done to them, whether they were on a long list of blackmail victims. I tried to cheer myself up by pretending I was a hero who saved those girls from Rafael's conniving schemes. But it didn't work. No matter what he did, I knew he didn't deserve to die. Heroes bring people to justice, not beat them up and fail to save them.

After the ceremony, I wandered through the crowded church, exploring the mix of emotions held by the funeral-goers. Some kids from school just thought it was cool to be there, since Rafael was so popular. His death made big news, and parents were already lobbying to have the "death trap" film set demolished. They all believed it was an accident, and nothing could have been done. I was the only person who knew that wasn't true. My brain played through hundreds of alternate endings for the night if I'd made different choices. I wish it would stop. I couldn't take back the choices I'd made.

There were a couple of guys I didn't know drifting through the funeral crowd, taking donations for some vague anti-teen-death charity. They looked like brothers. Both had the same cute, roguish charm. Their faces showed commiseration, but my powers told me they felt smug, the same kind of smug Rafael had felt as he pulled his trick. I wondered just what trick these two were up to. Every single person gave them money. A LOT of money. I watched with interest from a quiet corner.

Gavin, Rafael's best friend and blackmail confidant, found me there.

"You were with him, weren't you?" His voice was a growl.

I acted shocked. "Me and Rafael? Why would *he* have been somewhere with *me*?"

"I know he was going to meet you. You had something to do with him dying, I know it. You've been acting weird all week. Why were your hands all scratched up? What happened?"

He loomed over me. I saw anger in him, bubbling under his skin like the glow of lava. But now I knew what I could do with someone else's anger. I couldn't let him reveal to anyone

223

I was with Rafael that night. I had to scare him off and I had the power to do it.

"I don't know what you're talking about," I drawled. I rested a hand on the crossbar of a stone crucifix next to me. "But whatever happened to him could happen to you too if you don't keep quiet and leave me alone."

I squeezed my grip and the stone crumbled like chalk. The patter of the pieces falling to the floor was covered by the talking crowd. Gavin looked at me like the freak I was. My demonstration clearly had the desired effect.

Gavin ran away, leaving me with my regrets. Was I really a witch, or a monster? Was that the path I was fated for, using my powers for evil? I started to wonder how much I could achieve with my newfound abilities. Maybe, one way or another, I could still turn my life around.

The older boy with the donation bucket stared at me. I stared back, waiting for him to glance to my scar, be disgusted and turn away. My glare was a challenge.

But instead he smiled.

He came over and introduced himself. His name was Jake, and he was there with his little brother Jamie. They'd read about the funeral in the newspaper and came to see what donations they could get for their own "charitable cause".

"I saw what you just did," Jake whispered, dramatically low considering no one was interested in our conversation anyway. He kicked at the broken stone on the floor and raised his eyebrows.

"I didn't do anything. It was dodgy craftsmanship, broke on its own."

"You're a fast thinker, too. Perfect," he said. "Don't worry, I know what you can do, because I can do it, too. I'm so glad I spotted you. It's rare to find someone special, like us. How about we get out of here and talk more. Doesn't all this sadness give you a headache?"

I couldn't stop my eyes widening. "You really feel it too?"

Jake grinned. "The emotion reading, the super strength, the whole deal."

The idea of other people with powers like mine made a strong need for belonging bloom in my chest. My voice sounded way too vulnerable when I asked, "Can you help me understand what I am?"

"Sure. Come with me. I want to tell you how sticking by me will give you everything you ever wanted. Everything that people like us deserve."

Every nerve inside me ached to go with Jake, my body rebelling against my better judgment. Jake was charming and so handsome it made my palms sweaty. There was something downright supernatural about how tempting he was, but also something wrong and disturbing. I wouldn't fall for sweet talk again, and could already tell he wasn't one of the good guys.

I shook my head. "No. Go away. You're not my type."

Jake looked stunned. I doubt he got turned down... ever. He stared, assessing me again, his gaze lingering on my face.

He handed me a business card.

"What's this?" I asked.

"A gift, something I'm guessing is high on your wish list. I'll let Dr Rachenko know you're coming and to put any work on my tab. I've written my number on the back so you can get in touch again when you've seen what I can do for you."

I stared at the card. *Dr Rachenko- Discreet cosmetic surgery and enhancements.*

Jake tapped the card as I held it in my hands. "Everything you ever wanted starts here."

Jake called his brother over and the two of them left the building, counting the money they had been collecting from the grieving crowd. Definitely not on the good guy side.

I stared at what Jake had given me, my fingers clenched and shaking around the thin cardboard. Jake had offered me a new life, a new skin, and all I could wonder was what trick he would play on me, what catch this promise held. I couldn't stand the idea that his offer wasn't true.

And if the only catch was that I wouldn't be one of the good guys either, could I do that?

Deep inside I had always wanted to be something good and special, but it seems that I was born to be something other than a hero. I never had that sort of strength in me, the strength to stay beautiful on the inside. Ugliness had crawled inside me, driven in by the cruel words and games of my peers. It sat there, next to the dull ache I felt in my chest whenever my mind replayed the night at Siren's Haven. A montage it chose to replay often.

I shook the guilt and regret away, denying it. It didn't matter anymore. I would become beautiful on the outside. Everything I wanted, I would take. I had great plans. Operation: New Me, Mark II would not fail.

AUTHOR'S NOTE

When I decided to write Emma's backstory, I knew that it was going to be the tragic origin of a villain, rather than the normal hero's tale. That's the sort of story I'm used to writing, and that we're all used to reading- a person surmounting all the terrible trials thrown at them to become something better. In my mind, the difference between good people and bad people are the decisions they make in their darkest moments. Not everyone has it in them to rise above, and it's the ones that fall, that are beaten down, that tragically become villains. That's the story I wanted to explore in Emotionally Scarred. I don't want readers to think that Emma's actions are to be condoned, despite Rafael being not too nice himself. Emma has it in her to become a true super-villain. Will she, or will she have a chance to redeem herself?

Thanks for reading my short story, I hope you enjoyed it. You can read more about Emma and whether her "Operation: New Me, Mark II" plan succeeds and how she has to deal with what she's done in other books from the Empath Chronicles series.

A PERSONAL THANK YOU FROM SELINA

Thank you for reading my story, it means a lot to me to be sharing my magical worlds with you. As an indie author, receiving reviews and seeing people talk about my books are like receiving a big warm hug from my readers! Honest reviews help me improve as an author, and help bring my book to the attention of other readers. If you're enjoyed this book, please consider taking two minutes to leave a review at the online store you purchased this book. It really does mean the world to indie authors such as myself.

If you want to discuss the story or make sure I see your comments, just drop me an email at selina@selinafenech.com. I love to hear from readers, and reply to all personal emails!

ABOUT THE AUTHOR

Whether it's painting artworks or writing novels, creating fantasy works is Selina's biggest passion. She lives in Australia with her husband and daughter and loves food, gardening, geekery, and all things fantasy.

Find out more about Selina
Official website www.selinafenech.com
Facebook www.facebook.com/selinafenechart

www.ingramcontent.com/pod-product-compliance
Lightning Source LLC
Chambersburg PA
CBHW071603110726

47908CB00007B/2225